SAVAGE

A DIFFUSION TALE

STAN C. SMITH

Mbaiso
Production

To those who are compassionate. You are the future.

SAVAGE

Definition:

A fierce, brutal, or cruel person. An uncivilized human being.

If you have found this book,
the end of the world has already begun.

Are you prepared to face
what the new world might bring?

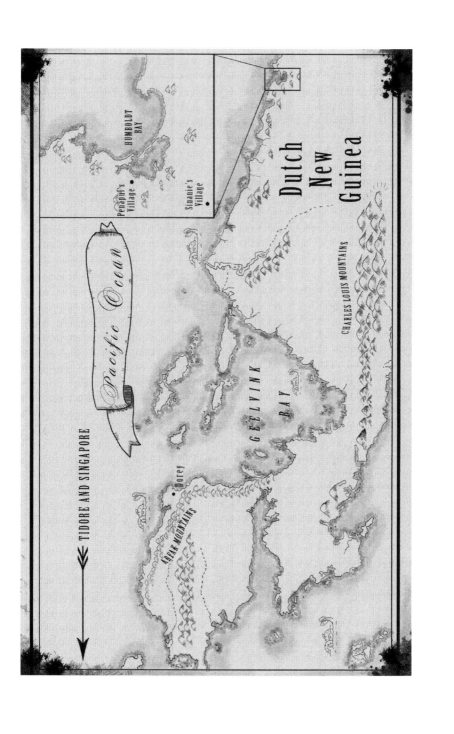

FOREWORD

by Peter Wooley
CEO, SouthPacificNet
Kembalimo designer

You are reading this book, which means the world as we know it is coming to an end.

Very few people know the name Samuel Inwood. Major players in the shaping of civilization rarely have the opportunity to live obscurely, though Samuel Inwood managed to do so. Now that this book is being published, Samuel's name will become well known around the globe.

For many years, Samuel Inwood did not want this book, his field journal, to be found. Why? Because he did not want the strange entity described within it to be found. However, if an object of such power does not wish to remain hidden, it will inevitably make itself known.

Diaries and journals are often recognized as historically significant. Leonardo da Vinci wrote thousands of pages of loosely organized thoughts and sketches, and his journals have fascinated and inspired people for over 500 years. Charles Darwin began his pocket journal habit as a naturalist aboard the HMS Beagle. His journals displayed a progression of ideas leading to a world-changing understanding of the origin of species by natural selection. Anne Frank's diary became an iconic work of literature that reminds us that a menacing layer of human nature exists dangerously close to the surface. The men of the Lewis and Clark expedition recorded more than a million words in their journals, offering a distinctive snapshot of the North American frontier. Years after the Lewis and Clark expedition, the men of the Burke and Wills expedition maintained journals, giving us a glimpse of inland Australia that at the time had been explored only by Aborigines.

These journals and many others help us see the personal side of historical events. They allow us to gaze into the past through the eyes of those who lived it, something history textbooks rarely do. The importance of each journal is determined by two factors. First, the significance of the events witnessed by the author. Second, the quality and thoroughness of the writing.

Regarding the first of these criteria, the events Mr. Inwood described in what is now Indonesian Papua will be considered by historians to be a pivotal turning point in human history. Whether the influences are for better or for worse is yet to be seen. Either way, the importance is undeniable.

Regarding the second criteria, Samuel's journal is detailed and coherent. I will point out, although the following text appears as one continuous journal, Samuel's original bound journal became filled with his words, forcing him to continue writing on various media available to him at the time, including the bark of trees. Eventually he gathered the fragments and transcribed them all into one book, often elaborating and filling in gaps from memory. For reasons described herein by Samuel himself, he was able to do this with flawless accuracy.

Mr. Inwood's transcribed journal is provided in its entirety. Because he intentionally structured it more like a book rather than field notes, the words have not been altered, other than changing certain spellings to more universally-accepted forms. Also, certain passages were removed to prevent revealing specific locations. Nothing is to be gained and much could be lost by encouraging throngs of curious onlookers to descend upon pristine wilderness and indigenous people who value their seclusion and traditional existence. Despite these warnings, some of you may set out to discover the indigenous tribe Samuel lived with for many years. If so, you will almost certainly fail. Should you succeed, you will probably never be seen again.

I have personally had the life-altering experience of visiting the wilderness region and indigenous people with whom Samuel spent so much of his life. There are only a few others who have, which is as it should stay. I have also had the honor of playing some small role in the more recent events unfolding as a result of Samuel's work. And so I have a rather exceptional perspective to offer you before you read this journal. My message is one of caution.

To loosely borrow from Einstein's thoughts on relativity, *all cultural diversity is relative.* Consider the diversity of human cultures. It is quite astounding, really, and Samuel's descriptions of several remote Papuan tribes further illustrate this. But with every passing decade, burgeoning transportation and communication technologies are transforming the planet into a global culture. These technologies accelerate cultural diffusion and homogenization. Customs, ideologies, and technologies are rapidly diffusing, resulting in blended and diluted cultures. It is not difficult to imagine the eventual consequence. Some of you will applaud this progression, reasoning that a global culture will facilitate communication and compassion and therefore reduce conflict. Others will condemn it as the tragic extinction of multitudes of unique and splendorous cultures and languages. I will not argue one way or the other, as this progression is inevitable either way.

Now let us consider things on a much larger scale, a task we have never had to do before. Whether you consider the human species to be richly diverse or one global culture, you must concede that we are all currently only one species. One human civilization. However, we now know there are other civilizations besides ours, with technological achievements far beyond our own. Cultural diffusion will likely continue on this larger, cosmic scale.

You may think we are walking a path into the future that is new to us. I urge you to be cautious and understand that we have walked similar paths before—on numerous occasions. The meeting of vastly different cultures has not always gone well, particularly for indigenous, less technological societies. Take a moment to ponder the implications.

There is much to be learned from the thoughts and actions of Samuel Inwood. He was a product of his time, and you may find some of his notions offensive by today's standards. Please look deeper. He seemed to have an uncanny understanding of the long-term consequences of his discoveries, and if he had acted differently it is quite possible none of us would be here today.

As always, our future is uncertain. And it is likely to be breathtaking. But rushing into it will not make it arrive sooner.

We would be wise to follow Mr. Inwood's example and take one restrained, vigilant step at a time.

Lastly, Mr. Inwood challenges us to look within ourselves. Are we compassionate beings? Many of us believe so, but I'm not so sure the state of our civilization verifies this. In the words of Samuel Inwood, we must all become improved.

— Peter Wooley

FEBRUARY 16, 1868

The Journal of Samuel Inwood
Transcribed by Mr. Inwood

L𝐸𝑇 it be known that I, Samuel Thaddeus Inwood, am not a man of the sea. It is with certainty that I make this claim, having spent the last seventy-four days aboard two steamers and a schooner on my journey from the port at Southampton to my current position in the great Pacific Ocean off the northern coast of New Guinea, Humboldt Bay being my final destination. Were you to lay eyes on the first ship of my voyage, the magnificent P&O steamship *Deccan*, you might think me a cowardly, unsturdy man. This ship carried me from England to the island of Singapore. Admittedly, the *Deccan* was a grand and impressive ship, with its long hall below the deck, the saloon. The saloon was comfortable, appointed with a large, ornately-carved table bolted to the floor, and every visible surface elegantly decorated with paint and gilt. But the meals served there, although numerous and of considerable size, were generally cold and plain. And the ship was crowded, with four berths per cabin and barely room to stand between them. Notwithstanding the ship's size, the motions of the sea produced constant rocking. This was accompanied by the ceaseless clanking of the engines, fueled by the labor of half-naked stokers shoveling coal into the furnaces.

During the first portion of this voyage, I found comfort only in the generous offerings, at no additional cost to me, of ale, porter, claret, port, and sherry. Champagne was even served twice a week. But finally, having decided to tour the engine rooms, which were open to the passengers, I discovered the ship's menagerie, a large compartment containing hundreds of animals, no doubt outnumbering the people on board. There were cows to provide milk, as well as pigs, sheep, chickens, and ducks. Notwithstanding the smell, I spent many hours there, perhaps more comfortably than in the company of my fellow travellers, although the collection of creatures steadily diminished as the ship's butcher converted them into meals for approximately three hundred passengers and crew.

As I have said, my cabin on the *Deccan* was small and barely tolerable. I can therefore scarcely imagine the conditions my assistant, Charles Newman, will endure when he travels to join me in the coming weeks. Due to the fortunate position of the family into which I was born, I was able to purchase a gentleman's first class ticket. Charles, I'm afraid, will be in possession of a servant's ticket, with its proportionably less elegant accommodations.

Upon arriving in Singapore, I went about procuring provisions, as I had been told that the islands I would encounter nearer to New Guinea would be lacking in articles often used by Europeans, particularly those used for cleanliness and comfort. After six days of searching and bartering for the items on my list, and then carefully packing them, I set off on a small screw steamer and made my way to the spice island of Tidore. This portion of my journey involved nine days living in wretched quarters. To pass the time, and to procure fresh sea air in order to escape the discomfort of seasickness, I spent many hours on the deck, watching innumerable islands pass. This had the effect of increasing my anticipation for arrival at my final destination, as each of the islands was covered with lofty and luxuriant forest. Beyond the shores of larger islands were hills and mountains, and I was told that few of these had ever been trodden by civilized men.

When I arrived at Tidore I endeavored to procure a meeting with the Sultan, who had been granted rights by the Dutch to much of the northern coast of New Guinea. I made the acquaintance of a Dutch trader there who assisted with arranging this meeting. The Sultan, a man of Malayan race, was eager to assist in any efforts that might result in trading colonies being established within his jurisdiction. He generously provided me a letter of authority to go where I pleased and receive every assistance I required. As an additional service, he assigned a lieutenant and a soldier to accompany me until I could establish myself. They were to provide my protection and assist with my relations with the natives at Humboldt Bay, who were generally known to be hostile.

I now find myself on the last portion of my journey, aboard the schooner Hester Helena. This is the same ship used by Alfred Wallace, who explored and collected specimens throughout the Malay Archipelago for eight years, from 1854 to 1862. Mr. Wallace's descriptions of his travels so inspired me that I sought out the occasion to introduce myself to him in London. I told him I was most determined to carry out a zoological and entomological study of the magnificent island of New Guinea, particularly a part of it he had not the opportunity to visit. The dear man immediately became interested and graciously agreed to provide any assistance he could. We met for dinner soon after that, and he provided valuable information beyond my expectations, including the name of the man who owned the Hester Helena, as well as a list of supplies I would need. I believe, in fact, that this trip would likely end in disaster were it not for his guidance.

My final destination, where I expect to arrive tomorrow, is Humboldt Bay. Mr. Wallace, during the eight years of his expedition, spent only a few months in New Guinea. He made residence at Dorey, on the western peninsula. Although he had greatly anticipated visiting New Guinea, he found Dorey to be disagreeable. He described the natives there as inferior to others in the region, both morally and physically. There was continual rain there, and he became quite ill. There was also a preponderance of abominable biting ants and blow-flies, which made his most trifling tasks wearisome. And all of this was uncompensated by any great success in collecting impressive specimens of birds or insects.

But Mr. Wallace had the fortunate opportunity to visit with a ship captain who had stayed several days at Humboldt Bay, some five hundred miles to the east of Dorey, just at the border of the western portion of New Guinea administered by the Dutch Government. The captain reported that Humboldt Bay was a much more agreeable place, more beautiful and with a better harbor. The natives there were shy and untrusting, and they were unsophisticated, having only been visited by occasional stray whalers and Bugis traders (industrious sailors from the large island of Celebes). Most intriguing was the observation that the natives wore as ornaments the most magnificent Bird of Paradise feathers. Only about eighteen species of Paradise Birds are known to exist, but I suspect there are more to be found, as well as new species of mammals and insects, by a naturalist willing to venture some distance inland. Which is exactly what I intend to do.

Hence it is with great anticipation that I now approach my final destination. Yet I also must admit to some amount of trepidation. Tribes of New Guinea's northern coast are known to be murderous savages, in the lowest stages of barbarism. And unlike my esteemed friend, Mr. Wallace, I have had few previous opportunities to dispose peaceable negotiations with such savages. It is quite possible that my expedition might end with a savage's arrow in my heart, or his knife across my throat as I sleep.

2

FEBRUARY 17, 1868

I ATTRIBUTE the success of our landing at Humboldt Bay, if not my very survival, to the rather large collection of goods for trade I purchased in Singapore. Following the advice of Alfred Wallace, I had visited the Chinese bazaar bearing a list of items that would be valued by indigenous Papuans. To my delight, in the hundreds of shops there, most of these things could be purchased more cheaply than they could be purchased in England. I procured an abundance of knives, hatchets, gimlets, rolls of quality calico, balls of white cotton thread, beads, tobacco, and bottles of Java rum made from the sap of coconut palms, called arrack. With somewhat more persistence, I also managed to purchase muskets, gunpowder, and a supply of Dutch copper cents (the 100th part of a guilder), in case these could also be traded.

As before stated, the natives of Humboldt Bay are known to be unfriendly. But I was encouraged by reports from the Hester Helena's captain that the place had been successfully visited by the Dutch on more than one occasion, and I was determined to make my residence and do my collecting there.

This morning the Hester Helena arrived at Humboldt Bay. It is a fine bay, with a long, narrow spit of land projecting out to the northwest, almost joining another spit projecting out to the southeast. This provides a narrow channel serving as an entrance to a well-protected bay with good anchorage for vessels. But there were no vessels to be seen when we arrived, other than a small prau. Praus are used throughout the Malay Archipelago and are recognized by having a single outrigger, which is almost as large as the main hull. This vessel was tied to a mangrove, its single sail loosely furled, and so I assumed it was owned by visiting Bugis traders.

I stood watching anxiously at the Hester Helena's prow as we passed between the spits of land. The main village suddenly came into my sight. Many of the houses were built standing completely in the water, upon posts, with long, crude bridges connecting them to the shore. More houses could be seen inland, also standing upon posts. All of the houses and bridges seemed to be placed with little or no regularity and were often crooked. Near the shore, but also standing in water, was a much larger structure with a domed roof rather like a boat's hull, perhaps a council-house. Among the houses were numerous posts rising from the water or land that did not support anything. As we sailed nearer, I saw that upon each of these posts was a human skull, upside down, with the crown of the skull fastened to the top of the post. Below the skulls, each post was roughly carved in the revolting shape of a naked human figure, some of them male, some female. The general appearance of the village was somewhat alarming, and I was most grateful for the company of the lieutenant and his soldier from Tidore.

Soon, more than a dozen Papuan men emerged from the houses carrying bows and arrows. Even from some distance I could see that many of them wore various necklaces of beads and cords, but they were very nearly in a state of nature, almost naked but for a peculiar long and brown cylinder arranged as a sheath upon the sexual organ. Each of the men wore an impressive mop of frizzly hair upon his head, as well as a beard of the same frizzly nature. Unlike the Malay lieutenant and his soldier, with their lighter skin and less prominent features, these men were obviously true Papuans, with deep brown or even black bodies. Their stature was tall, equally as tall as an average European man, and they were handsome and well-made, with the result of making them seem all the more threatening when they began shouting and shaking their bows at us.

The captain gave the order to cast anchor at a safe distance, and I boarded the ship's tender, along with the lieutenant and soldier from Tidore and three Dutch crewmen, with the intention of landing. This, however, provoked even more shouting and gesticulations from the natives, and some of them began nocking their arrows and bending their bows, implying that they would shoot at us if we rowed closer.

Having anticipated such a reception, I had raided my supply of goods I had purchased for trade. I now hastily wrapped some knives and handkerchiefs in a length of calico printed with a fine floral pattern and threw the bundle to the natives. We then gave way and lay at anchor for some minutes while they inspected the gifts. We approached them again, and I threw another bundle, this one containing a bottle of arrack and some tobacco. Again, we gave way and waited. The next time we approached, they beckoned us to land the tender.

Once we arrived on shore, they seemed to have lost all

their will for hostile threats. They approached us with curiosity, some of them now seeming even timid. They inspected my clothing and took particular interest in my spectacles and boots. Four or five men tried my spectacles in succession, and they laughed with boisterous merriment, seemingly surprised that they could not see through them. One of the men wore a great deal more ornaments in his hair than the others, as well as several impressive necklaces of animal teeth alternating with black and white beads. He also wore, at the top of each arm, a wide strap of woven grass, to which were attached numerous long black feathers of some unknown bird. I assumed this man to be the village chief, and I handed him yet another bundle containing tobacco and arrack. This brought a good many smiles from the men, and soon our assemblage on the shore grew as women and other men emerged from the houses.

The women were somewhat less handsome than the men. They were completely naked, other than wearing necklaces and earrings. But these were arranged in elegant ways, with the ends of the necklaces being attached to the earrings, and then draped in loose loops around the back of the head and fastened to a carefully knotted mound of hair. Their necklaces and earrings were composed of animal teeth, beads, and lengths of silver and copper wire. This exceedingly tasteful ornamentation greatly improved their rather barbarous appearance.

While standing in the midst of these natives, I began to fully appreciate their savage nature. The tallest of them exceeded my own height, and upon their bodies were numerous scars and deformities apparently due to fighting, perhaps with rival tribes. Most of them carried bows, knives, or sharpened wooden spears, and they handled these with a comfortable ease, as if they had used them since childhood. Due to the height and boisterous behavior of these natives, the smaller stature and reserved, almost bashful Malay character of the lieutenant and his soldier assigned to my protection at once seemed to me to be distressingly unsatisfactory. I therefore became doubly determined to establish peaceable relations and was glad for my substantial collection of goods for trade.

It quickly became clear that communication was going to be a problem. The lieutenant and his man did not understand the tribe's language, nor did the three Dutch crewmen who had come ashore with us. Furthermore, they informed me that no one else on the Hester Helena would know the language. But the Papuans soon resorted to gesticulations as if they were accustomed to dealing with visitors who could not speak their language. I set about trying to explain that I wished to bring my supplies to shore and go about setting up my residence there, but as my arms grew tired from gesticulating, and the natives repeatedly shook their heads in confusion, I began to fear that this was beyond my ability to convey.

To my great relief, two Bugis traders, who did indeed own the prau that was moored to the mangroves nearby, came to my aid. The men, who had emerged from a house wiping their eyes as if they had only just awoke, could speak Malay, the semi-barbarous language of the lieutenant from Tidore, and they also knew a little of the language of the Papuan tribe. Even I could understand some of what the Bugis men said, as I had spent significant time learning Malay aboard the screw steamer from Singapore and the Hester Helena, knowing that it was the most widely spoken language throughout the Malay Archipelago. I was not at all surprised that the Papuan tribe would have their own dialect. I understood that such striking fragmentation of language among these people was an example of their low state of civilization. Villages only a few miles distant from each other were known to speak different dialects or entirely different languages, so that communication between tribes was nearly impossible. And I had read that this barrier to communication was made worse by the hostile nature of some Papuan tribes, who often raided neighboring villages, murdering the men and capturing the women and children, assimilating them into their own tribe.

The Bugis traders explained to us that they visited Humboldt Bay regularly to exchange goods for furs and Birds of Paradise, which were highly valued for their magnificent feathers and in fact were an article of commerce. They seemed incredulous of my desire to reside with the Papuans but were eager to offer to return periodically to sell me goods I might need. I took some comfort in this, knowing that the Hester Helena will not return for a month, when it will bring my assistant, Charles Newman. After that, it will not return to pick us up until three years have passed. Since Humboldt Bay is hardly known and rarely visited, and the lieutenant and his soldier are to return to Tidore by way of a Bugis trading prau, it could therefore be three years before another European vessel enters the bay.

Notwithstanding their doubts about my plans, the Bugis men took considerable care to explain to the natives that I desired to stay with them in order to study the animals, birds, and insects of the region. This resulted in shaking of heads among the Papuans, and even laughter. But when told that I would be collecting specimens, including Birds of Paradise, the laughter stopped. They seemed suspicious of this, as if it were an intrusion upon their rights. I produced my letter of authority from the Sultan of Tidore. The Bugis traders explained what it was, but this seemed to anger the natives even more. Finally, I gave the man I assumed was the village chief the last pouch of tobacco I had brought from my supply on the ship and told the natives I was willing to pay them in goods or Dutch copper cents for any assistance they would afford me. I told them, in fact, that I was interested in employing three or four of them to assist me with building my house and with shooting and collecting specimens. This news seemed to interest them, as it was followed by a great deal of arguing among the younger men and boys and jostling of each other as if they desired to be first in line to become employed. I attempted to continue my explanation so that the matter could be resolved and I could then proceed to unloading my baggage and goods, but they had become so distressed over this that there could be no going on until a decision was made as to who would be hired to assist me. I chose three young men who appeared to be sturdy, healthy specimens. This resulted in yet another round of boisterous talk and jostling, but fortunately it was with good-natured smiles.

And so at last my baggage and goods were brought to shore. The Hester Helena then made a hasty departure, as the captain had other business to attend to. I will admit that I watched the ship leave the bay with some consternation, as my future and my success here seemed quite uncertain.

The Bugis traders told us they would be departing soon, and they kindly offered the house they had built near the village, which they used when they visited. The lieutenant and soldier assigned to my protection immediately accepted this offer. Aboard the Hester Helena, however, I had been subjected to the most alarming snoring from one of them as they slept, so I was determined to begin constructing my own house.

The village chief himself, whose name I learned was Penapul, took some interest in helping me select a location for my house. After some talking, which was assisted by the Bugis men, I realized that Penapul had assumed I would want to build a house over the water. However, I was disinclined to do so, having just spent so many days at sea.

I asked why some of the houses were built over water while others were built over land. The villagers were astonished that I would not know, and they explained that this arrangement was designed to help defend the village from raiding tribes. Some tribes would attack from the water, approaching the village in canoes. In this case the women and children were moved to the houses built some distance up the side of the hill, and the raiders were fought at the shore to prevent them from landing. However, some tribes might attack from the land, in which case the women and children would be moved to the houses built over the water, and again the raiders were fought at the shore, but in this case to prevent them from entering the water.

I also learned that defense from attacking tribes was the very reason their houses were built on posts some six to eight feet above ground or water. I had to admit that it seemed it would be much easier to kill a man whose hands were otherwise occupied with the task of climbing.

The human skulls fastened high on posts were intended to demonstrate to raiding tribes that Penapul's tribe was to be feared. The skulls were apparently from slain attackers. I asked if the village was raided often. Penapul laughed at this and assured me that I need not worry. Even had I been sure he correctly understood my question, I could hardly have found comfort in his answer.

Finally I was shown several possible locations for building a house. I chose one that was on elevated ground, near a path often used by the Papuans to walk from the village to the forest, and not too far from a stream for washing and for fresh water. The place was only about a hundred yards from the shore, and I planned to have a window from which I could look at the sea as I worked.

In Tidore I had purchased a good many cadjans, water-proof mats made of interwoven pandanus palm leaves, to be used to cover my belongings to protect them from rain, and then eventually to be used as roofing material for my house. I had my new laborers move my baggage and goods to the place where I would build, and we covered them with the cadjans.

It would take several days to build a proper house, so I attempted to get my boys to help me construct a rough shelter in which to sleep during the process. However, by this time the Bugis traders were not to be seen, and I had to resort to gesticulating and pantomiming each task that I wanted accomplished. This became wearisome and did not work to my satisfaction. Just as I was thinking of giving up, the oldest of my four workers, a boy of perhaps eighteen, named Amborn, waved for me to follow him. He took me to the house where he slept, which was actually little more than a hut. Upon entering it I saw that two smoke-dried human skulls were suspended from the eaves. Amborn pointed to a sleeping mat, which I assumed was his. I was unwilling to sleep in his bed, but I did agree to temporarily share his roof. I went to my things, fetched some blankets, and arranged them in a corner. There were two other sleeping mats in the house, and I soon discovered that Amborn shared the house with two boys about his age. When I have the capability and opportunity, I will inquire if this is a normal custom of these people.

And so, as the light of the day fades, I am preparing to spend my first night upon the shore of the great island of New Guinea. I am quite pleased with the progress made today, although I will sleep with a loaded gun beside me, as I am uncertain of the natives' intentions.

3

FEBRUARY 22, 1868

ANTS AND MOSQUITOES plagued me terribly during that first night, after which I fashioned a rough wooden bedstead and applied a lavish layer of palm oil to its legs to stop the ants from climbing up to roam at will over every inch of my body. I also located my mosquito curtain in my stores and affixed it above my temporary bed. This allowed me to sleep in much more comfort, although the bites on my face, ankles, and wrists from the first night resulted in ceaseless irritation for several days.

For four days I was occupied from sunrise to dark with constructing my house. Notwithstanding the assistance I got from my boys and the two men from Tidore, several confounding complications obstructed the process. First, the Bugis traders had sailed away in their prau on the very morning I began construction, and I was left to whatever communication efforts I could muster on my own in conveying my needs to my three Papuan helpers. This meant I had to energetically pantomime every small task I wanted them to carry out.

Second, the villagers could scarcely believe that I desired to build my house with the floor just above the ground. They seemed to think this arrangement would certainly result in my being murdered by a raiding tribe, and I soon concluded that I could not convince them otherwise. Hence we began construction by digging holes and embedding poles tall enough to support a floor that was eight feet high and walls that were another eight feet beyond that. The result of this was that every minor building task required us to carefully position ladders and supports in such a way that we could safely work without falling.

Procuring suitable building materials was the third hindrance. I had initially assumed I would collect sturdy corner poles and bamboo from the forest near the village, and I had brought axes and choppers for that purpose. However, the villagers explained, through extensive gesticulations, that bamboo and poles had to be carried long distances, as the supply near the village had already been exhausted. At one end of the village was a large pile of materials the villagers had collected for building houses. Hence I had to pay the village chief for what I needed. I offered Dutch copper cents as payment, only to discover that the Papuans had no interest in coins. I will have to use them to purchase goods from the Bugis traders upon their return, as they are of no use to me here.

Yet another hindrance to building my house was the apparent laziness of my Papuan laborers. Without exception, I would have to begin working each morning alone. I would then soon be joined by the two soldiers from Tidore, and the native boys would gradually arrive, apparently at whatever time they felt inclined to. They would often arrive without the choppers I had given to them specifically for the work to be done. They seemed quite content to stand about and watch my progress, not performing any tasks until I made efforts to pantomime what I wished them to do. Often, all three of them would engage in a task that could easily be done by only one or two.

But progress was made, although gradually. We built the house roughly square, about fifteen feet by fifteen feet, with a floor of bamboo, walls covered with ataps (woven mats made of sago leaves I had bought from the natives), and a roof made from the cadjans I had purchased in Tidore. I constructed a small bamboo table at which I could work, with an atap secured upon it to provide a smooth surface. I then positioned it so that I would have a view of the sea through the door. Next to the house we built a bench and another table, with a slanted roof above it, where meals could be prepared and where we could skin and prepare collected birds, mammals, and insects. We cleared away brush and a few trees to allow the breeze from the bay to cool the house. Finally, I had my boys assist with moving my baggage and stores inside. I was especially grateful for their help with this, as each item had to be hoisted up an eight-foot ladder.

The height of my house caused me some concern. I am a rather restless sleeper and have even occasionally awakened only to find myself in a place some distance from where I began my night's sleep. Fearing that I might stumble about in a nocturnal state of half-sleep and fall to the ground, I made a rope latch on the door to secure it at night.

We completed my house yesterday afternoon. By that time I had already learned a few words of the language of the village, and I dismissed my boys for the day and asked them to return in the morning. I then constructed a more permanent bedstead of bamboo, attached my mosquito curtain, and applied palm oil to each of the legs to impede the ants. Thus I experienced a most restful night, having well established myself in my own house.

This morning, as I had grown to expect, my boys arrived gradually, having no apparent inclination to promptness or labor. I then set about teaching them the skills of collecting and preparing specimens. I determined that Amborn, the oldest, was best suited to handle a gun, and I taught him to shoot. First I instructed him on pouring in the powder in amounts appropriate for shooting balls at animals such as opossums or tree kangaroos, and for shooting number eight shot at birds. When we proceeded to shooting, the noise of this brought a good portion of the villagers to watch, and they were greatly entertained by watching Amborn try to hit the targets I provided.

In order to teach my other boys, named Miok and Loo, to skin birds, I needed specimens. This was of no difficulty, because as soon as Amborn became skilled at hitting targets of paper and wood, he took it upon himself to shoot every bird he saw. Soon I had a small collection of common birds, and I had to take the gun from Amborn's hands to avoid having more than needed.

The skinning of birds hardly needed to be taught, as these natives were already skilled at hunting and preparing their game for eating. Hence I needed only to demonstrate how to carefully scrape all vestiges of flesh away to prevent spoiling, and to fasten tags upon which I could then write the appropriate identifying information.

In the coming days, I shall go into the forest with my boys for my first attempts at procuring more rare and unusual specimens.

4

MARCH 6, 1868

I MUST FIRST PROVIDE some contextual foundation before I describe the events of the previous two weeks. As I have said before, the feathers of certain birds, as well as the skins of some mammals, are used throughout the Malay Archipelago as articles of commerce. The chiefs of coastal villages acquire dried skins of various parrots, cockatoos, and particularly Birds of Paradise from inland mountain tribes and give them to Bugis and Ceram traders in exchange for goods such as knives, arrack, and tobacco. Also, since the north coast tribes are under the rule of the Sultan of Tidore, a certain number of Paradise Bird skins are owed to the Sultan each year as a form of tribute. The local villagers, therefore, have a somewhat hostile attitude regarding the collection and trading of feathers and skins in the area near their village. I can imagine two reasons they might have adopted this attitude. First, since they trade goods to the inland tribes for these feathers and skins, they might (fairly) presume that any person, me specifically, who buys these directly from the inland tribes will pay a higher price, thus resulting in a higher price being demanded by the inland tribes at all times. Second, they might (incorrectly) presume that I will take the items I purchase to the Sultan, who in turn will then continue to demand more of such goods for his annual payment of tribute. Being naturally lazy and disinclined to engage in labor beyond the minimum necessary, it is no surprise that they strongly resist any action that might result in greater demands upon them.

Having taught my boys to shoot and prepare specimens, on February 24 I had them accompany me on my first extensive collecting excursion away from the village. We shot a few nice birds, including several types of pigeons, honeysuckers, and parrots, as well as common small and plain varieties. Upon our return, these were skinned and prepared to my specifications.

Feeling as if things were going quite well, including my ability to communicate, on the following day I explained to my boys that I wished to be taken to the nearest tribe known to collect Birds of Paradise, so that I might purchase some. I had not yet collected any of these most desired birds and hoped that the area near Humboldt Bay would produce species new to European collections. I was careful not to mention this request until the day for which I had planned this excursion, so that my boys would be obliged to do this before they could speak of it to the other villagers. When they understood my request, they glanced at each other uneasily but did not protest.

The walk to the inland village required some climbing, but it was not exceedingly difficult, and we arrived after about two hours, in which I would guess we travelled three miles. The villagers there looked similar to those of my host tribe, although their ornamentations included very few metals or elements that would need to be brought from more civilized places. They gathered around me to inspect my clothing, pale skin, and spectacles, in much the same way that Penapul's tribe had done the day I had arrived at Humboldt Bay. They probably had even fewer opportunities to see white men, if indeed they had seen any at all. We were guided to one of the houses, and there I saw human skulls hanging from the rafters. I wondered if these were collected from the same tribes that were enemies of Penapul's tribe. Or perhaps some of them actually were from Penapul's tribe, as I had come to realize in recent days, due to my discussions with Amborn, that the occasional raiding of villages seemed to be a natural part of life here, and was not an act that would preclude friendly trading between tribes.

These villagers regularly provided feathers and skins to the Humboldt Bay tribe, who in turn exchanged some of them for goods from the Bugis traders and gave some of them to the Sultan of Tidore as annual payment of tribute. When my boys explained to them what I wished to purchase, they were delighted, and soon I had numerous dried skins of Paradise Birds from which to choose. Some of the birds were poorly prepared and not suitable for my needs, and all but one of them were the common yellow type. The other was a magnificent specimen, of a type that I thought might be new to science. It had a head of yellow and black, but the body was covered in feathers of rust brown and orange, with the most remarkable lengthened, bright orange feathers protruding from the body behind the wings. This skin was well preserved, likely because the Papuans knew it would bring a higher price. I selected three of the common type and the rare orange one. Not knowing what goods the natives would value, I had brought a variety of items, but they were most interested in knives and choppers, and were quite willing to accept only a few of these for the birds. I had Amborn ask them if they would be willing to collect more types of Paradise Birds for me to purchase from them, and this resulted in enthusiastic nodding of their heads and waving of their new knives and choppers.

I was pleased with the day's success and believed this to be a promising trading arrangement with the mountain tribe.

But this was not to be, for on the next day, Penapul, having heard the circumstances of my trading with the neighboring tribe, arrived at my house with a group of tribesmen, including my three boys. He was in a frightful state of agitation, and my first thought was that they had come to add my skull to their collection. Penapul repeatedly pointed in the direction of the mountain village, indicating his disapproval of my previous day's trading. He then turned to Amborn, who was now making an effort to avoid looking directly at me, apparently torn between the words of his chief and his loyalty to me. After some excited words between them, Amborn explained to me, with words and gesticulations, that he was to fetch the birds I had procured the day before and turn them over to Penapul. I was reluctant to allow him to do this, but I had no intention of giving up my head for such a cause, as I am quite fond of it.

At this point the lieutenant and soldier from Tidore arrived. I explained in Malay what was happening. The two men then confronted the natives, threatening them with their guns. The dispute was quickly becoming alarming, which was likely made worse by their incapability to properly communicate. Finally I had to place myself between them to protect the men whose purpose was actually to protect me. I simply stood between them with my hands held before me, hoping the natives would recognize the respect due to a civilized man, until things became quiet. Reluctantly, I went into my house and selected two of the common yellow Paradise Birds and gave them to Penapul, hoping he did not know of the other two. He nodded at this, apparently satisfied, and soon he and his tribesmen left me alone with the lieutenant and soldier. The lieutenant told me it would be best if he and his man were to guard my house whenever I left it again to go collecting, as the Papuans would surely try to steal my belongings upon the first opportunity to do so. I rather doubted the threat to be that extreme, but I agreed, as the two men had no other purpose here but to protect and assist me, and this would keep them safely occupied some distance from the villagers, thus avoiding further conflict.

I made a few moderately successful collecting excursions in the area near my house during the two days following, and on the third day I instructed Amborn to again take me to the mountain village. I had every legal right to do this, with the proper letter of authority, and after several days of pondering the injustice of my situation, I made the decision with confidence. To my surprise, Amborn agreed to take me there. I asked the lieutenant to guard my house, and we then departed. However, when we arrived at the village, there were no friendly greetings, and we were told they had not been successful hunting and therefore had no specimens to trade. When asked if they would have some soon, they just shook their heads. I could only assume that Penapul's tribesmen had gone to the mountain tribe to warn them to avoid trading with me. This would explain why Amborn was willing to take me there.

I returned to the Humboldt Bay village frustrated and with no specimens other than a few common birds we had shot while walking. To add to my difficulties, I arrived at my house to discover it abandoned by the lieutenant and soldier. Thinking they might be sleeping or eating, I went to the hut where they resided, but they were not there, nor were their belongings. I returned to my house to enlist the help of Amborn, who was busy skinning the birds we had shot. I took him to the lieutenant's hut and used my limited vocabulary to tell him I wished to know their whereabouts. I then took him to find the chief, and with much gesticulating and talking, I was told that a trader had arrived while I was inland, and that the lieutenant and soldier had decided to return to Tidore aboard the trader's prau. This explanation seemed to me to be suspicious. Firstly, the lieutenant had said nothing to me in regards to leaving at the next opportunity. Secondly, it seemed unusual that the trader would arrive, conduct his business, and then depart within such a brief time. But no amount of questioning could produce any further explanation that might settle my doubts.

In the days following, it seemed as if many of the villagers went to some trouble to avoid my presence, often looking at the ground when passing by, or even turning to walk a different path when seeing me approaching.

In the days leading up to today, I adequately occupied my time by doing some collecting near my house, returning frequently to be sure my property was not being stolen. Continuing this limited habit, however, would never have allowed me to substantially expand my collection, and so I had nearly succeeded in convincing myself that my fears were unfounded, and that I should again begin travelling inland to collect.

My fears, however, were rekindled today. I paid a visit to the chief, Penapul, to purchase some bamboo and wood poles to build next to my house a small hut that would be better suited for preparing meals. Upon entering his house my attention was drawn, as it usually was, to the impressive collection of human skulls hanging from the eaves. On previous visits I had counted eight, at least four more than any of the other houses I had visited. But today there were ten, two of which appeared to be freshly prepared, with gleaming white bones and bits of red tissue still attached in various hard-to-clean notches and crevices.

I will endeavor to find evidence that the two new skulls in Penapul's hut belonged to my men from Tidore, but I suspect that such evidence would provide me no further comfort or protection. For that, I will continue to have a loaded gun at my side.

5

APRIL 4, 1868

My assistant, Charles Newman, arrived two days ago on the Hester Helena. When the ship arrived, the villagers proceeded to give it the same unfriendly and threatening welcome they had given me, but I was able to convince them that more gifts would be given if they would yield.

Charles stepped from the ship's tender to the shore wearing a black coat over a black waistcoat and white shirt, looking altogether uncomfortable and misplaced. Although thirty-four years old, his diminutive stature, wavy black hair, and sprightly bearing made him appear much younger. The indigenes were curious about Charles, but if they held suspicions about his purpose here, they did not reveal them, nor did they threaten him once he was upon the shore. When they surrounded him to inspect his strange clothing, he nearly disappeared in their midst, though I occasionally glimpsed his fearful eyes as he attempted to look to me for reassurance that he was not about to be run through with a chopper or spear.

At last the natives gave way, and I was able to embrace him and then shake his hand, which I did most vigorously.

"I am as pleased as all creation to stand at last on the shore of New Guinea." Charles said. "I trust that things have gone well for you here."

"Well, I still have my skull, at least for now," said I.

He frowned at this, so I laughed and told him we would discuss it later. We then occupied ourselves with unloading his possessions, and I talked for some time with the schooner's captain.

Even I can scarcely believe that, as a man of good breeding and some intelligence, I did not load my things onto the ship and travel with Charles to a less threatening location. Indeed I did consider it, and the ship's captain even encouraged me to do so. But I was overcome by an odd and perhaps unwise sense of resolve to surmount the adversity of my current station. I felt that if I were to give up and leave Humboldt Bay, I would be forced to consider a failure the mission I had dreamed and planned for so long. And I was encouraged by the unencumbered enthusiasm of my dear assistant, Charles, who seemed even more delighted to be here than I had been when I first arrived.

The villagers gradually retreated to their houses and previous tasks, leaving us alone by the shore. With Charles at my side, I watched the Hester Helena sail from Humboldt Bay, hoping we would still be alive upon its return three years hence.

"Sir," Charles said, breaking the silence, "you are the author of my delight. I am here at your will, and I can scarcely express enough gratitude. Since I was a boy I have dreamed of sharing in the glory seen by stalwart explorers of such wild places." He turned to face the inland and raised his hands. "And this, sir, is the wildest of them all."

I laughed, having nearly forgotten the extent of Charles'

enthusiasm, kindness of disposition, and fondness for well-spoken words. "It is I who would thank you," said I. "My stay here has been less than fruitful, but with your assistance I will soon remedy the situation."

Charles straightened his back, as if to become taller. "Sir, by my honor, which is bright and unsullied, I am at your service."

I introduced Charles to my boys, and we had them move his baggage into the house, which was now getting rather full. We then found Penapul and gave him a bottle of arrack in exchange for some bamboo, which we used to construct a bedstead for Charles, similar to my own. I insisted that Charles sleep in my house until we had the opportunity to build a second house adjacent to it.

Charles had brought me several letters from my mother and father, and from my beloved Lindsey. Before I had left England, Lindsey had agreed to marry me upon my return, which was to be no more than four years after my departure, and I took great pleasure in reading her letters. There was even a letter from Alfred Wallace, offering me encouragement and a few words of advice that he had forgotten to mention when we had met. Charles then told me, with characteristic humor and oratory skill, of his travels. He had actually enjoyed his time on each of the ships, indicating that he was rather more suited to life upon the sea than I had been, which made me feel less troubled over purchasing a servant's ticket for him.

Only after I had sent my boys home for the day, and it was late in the evening, did I finally explain all the details of my disagreeable situation to him. I found his words regarding this to be encouraging.

NOTE: When transcribing this notebook, I determined that writing some of the conversations exactly as they took place would help readers understand the decisions that were made leading up to subsequent fateful events. Below is the conversation that took place after I had explained to Charles all that had happened. Due to Charles' penchant for colloquialisms, I have added, parenthetically, a few translations.

"I CERTAINLY SEE why you are in such a state of hugger-mugger (confusion)," said Charles. "Perhaps the simplest explanation is that the soldiers from Tidore had grown weary of the place and did indeed take advantage of a trading prau that happened to arrive on the very day you visited the mountain tribe. I would have gone to the Sultan of Tidore to inquire as to whether they had safely returned to their stations there, had I known there was such a need."

"Yes, it is possible that they left on a trading vessel," said I. "But I find the entire situation to be troubling nevertheless. While the Hester Helena was here today, I asked Captain Duivenboden if he had heard any news of the two men returning to Tidore, but he had heard nothing."

"Which by no means proves anything one way or the other," said he.

"Quite true."

After thinking quietly for some time, Charles said, "Perhaps we should pocket the native chief's affronts to your rights and consider things from his perspective."

"Go on."

"Penapul believes that he holds the rights to trading in the area surrounding his village, notwithstanding true and legal control being granted to the Sultan of Tidore. I imagine Penapul loves the Sultan as the Devil loves holy water, and no doubt he has fought to maintain his trading rights for many years. In his eyes this may be as precious to him as your rights as an English gentleman are to you. But you wish to collect birds and animals in the area—*his* area. You do not wish to trade the specimens you collect, nor to hinder in any way his trading of feathers and skins, but it seems likely you would not convince him of such truth."

"All of which is correct," I said. "So where does this lead your thoughts?"

"Perhaps we should appear to Penapul that we are willing to come out at the little end of the horn (disadvantaged), when in fact we may come out at the big end. We should promise to him that we will not trade with the mountain tribes." He held up his hand as I started to speak. "Yes, even though you have legal authority to do so. We should attempt to ask him which specific birds and mammals he does not wish us to collect, and thus we avoid them and remain in his favor. Or perhaps we should ask how far we would need to travel, or if there are any specific areas such as certain mountains or valleys, where he would not object to our collecting."

I considered this. "I suppose you are correct, although avoiding certain birds and mammals would be less than ideal, as it would result in a collection that does not truly represent the area's diversity of creatures."

"You are correct, sir," said Charles. "But I do wish to see some of the great island of New Guinea before I lay down the knife and fork. I am merely suggesting that we first gain the chief's favor, and then the fat may burn itself out of the fire (the trouble may blow over)."

Notwithstanding the serious nature of our conversation, I was compelled to laugh, as it had been many weeks since I had enjoyed the company of another civilized man.

"Assuming that the fat does indeed burn itself out of the fire," said I, "there will be much for us to accomplish in the coming months. Tell me, Charles, of your state of pleasurable excitement, as I am in need of words to remind me of why I endeavored to come here."

This resulted in a broad smile upon his face. "I fear that you may grow weary of my smirking gigglemug. My being here is like a childhood dream come true. You will be pleased to know that, before departing London, I finished putting up and labeling your substantial collection of beetles from Scotland. So I departed mad as hops (excitable), with no unfinished business to burden my mind. And now that I am here, in spite of my greeting by men who are clearly as savage as a meat axe, I am all-fired grateful for such an opportunity, and I am at your service, bag and baggage."

THE NEXT MORNING when my boys arrived to begin working on a house for Charles, I took Amborn with me to see the chief. With the boy's help I explained to Penapul that I wished to avoid interfering with or intruding upon his trading rights and asked if there might be places we could collect without doing so. He smiled broadly at this and immediately told me of a place where I was welcome to collect anything I wished. He made it abundantly clear that there were many birds and other animals there, and of types that were not to be found near the village. This was quite satisfactory to me, until I asked how far it was. Apparently it required several days of travelling, which meant Charles and I would have to sleep in the forest, without the comforts I had taken no small effort to create in my house. Penapul assured me that my boys would take me there, presumably helping with carrying and with other tasks.

It did somewhat surprise me that Penapul was so pleased to offer this assistance, but any uncertainties I may have had were lessened by my excitement to begin serious collecting efforts again and my hopes of being in the chief's good favor, which in turn would ensure our safety.

Although I returned to my house with renewed enthusiasm, I still insisted that Charles and I both sleep with loaded guns beside us.

6

APRIL 16, 1868

THE CONSTRUCTION OF CHARLES' house went without difficulties. It was, in fact, a more efficient process than the
construction of my own house, as I had become much more
skillful in conveying to my laborers what I wished for them to
do, due to my increasing command of their crude language
and of particular gesticulations they understood. We built the
house next to mine, at the same height above the ground,
although somewhat smaller. The construction took fewer than
three days, and this time seemed to pass quickly due to
Charles' interminable fervor.

After the house was complete I endeavored to teach
Charles all I had learned regarding the natives, guarding
against irritating insects, avoiding certain foods I had found to
cause intestinal distress, and other important necessities for
living here. I also provided Charles with a systematic review
of insects, birds, and other animals I had collected thus far,
which was miserably limited.

Finally, we began preparing for an excursion to the region
recommended to us by the chief. In preparing the necessary

supplies, my boys, Amborn in particular, were very helpful. They demonstrated how we could combine my limited supply of cotton canvas with natural materials from the forest to construct reasonably dry shelters that could be swiftly dismantled and carried for some miles to be erected again for the following night. It was beginning to look like we would be able to travel to the area and collect there for a number of days with acceptable comfort. Furthermore, I was able to make certain that my three boys could carry all necessary equipment and supplies. Charles and I would carry guns, ready to shoot birds and mammals when they were found.

On several occasions during these recent preparations, the chief came to see us. Upon each visit he excitedly gesticulated and talked about the distant region he had informed me about. It was as if he greatly anticipated our departure for the place, and he expressed exaggerated surprise that we had not already travelled there and returned with all manner of rare and magnificent creatures. I was at the same time encouraged and distressed by this newly-acquired attitude of jubilant support. Such copious enthusiasm was not typical for Penapul, and I could not help but find it to be suspicious.

My distress regarding this matter increased yesterday, when Penapul paid us yet another visit. He came to us at a time when my boys were not present, but my rapidly growing ability to communicate allowed me to understand much of what he was saying. He explained that he now wished for my three boys to guide us to the recommended region and then return to the village, leaving us there to collect and manage all necessary tasks on our own. He made it clear that the boys would return to us after an agreed upon number of days and then guide us and carry our supplies back. This arrangement was not satisfactory to me, which I attempted to explain to him. He either did not comprehend or was simply unwilling to discuss it further, for he promptly left us to puzzle over this news.

Last evening, after I had sent my boys away for the day, I discussed this new predicament with Charles.

NOTE: Again I have included this conversation exactly as it took place, to help readers understand the decisions that were made leading up to subsequent fateful events.

I WAS EXTREMELY DISTRESSED by our situation, and I paced back and forth in my house, slapping at mosquitoes with more force than necessary. "My instinct tells me I should fear the worst, that perhaps Penapul has instructed the boys to murder us in our sleep and return to the village."

As soon as I had uttered this, I knew it was not logical, and Charles confirmed this.

"If that were the case, sir, why tell us anything that might cause our suspicion? And for that matter, why not simply murder us here?"

"Well, for one thing, they know we keep our guns with us at all times. But I suppose you are correct. I cannot imagine, however, why he would wish for my boys to leave us in the wilderness. Perhaps he plans to stop them from returning for us, thinking we will perish without their assistance, thus being rid of us without any risk to members of his tribe."

Charles nodded at this.

"God blind me!" I cried. "We should have left this wretched place on the Hester Helena."

"Is it possible, sir, that you are allowing the chief to become your bugaboo?" asked Charles. "Perhaps we should not worry so much. Since my arrival here, I feel that I have come to know your boys quite well, particularly Amborn. They seem to have substantial loyalty to you, and now perhaps to me as well. And the chief seems to me to have a fancy for putting on the pot (being grand) and is rather impulsive, sometimes becoming excited about one idea or another and then promptly forgetting it in favor of yet another idea that seems interesting for the moment."

"Again you are correct, Charles. I believe I know what you are suggesting, that we proceed with our plans. When we arrive at or destination, we convince my boys to remain with us as we collect."

Charles continued my reasoning. "And when we return, Penapul will either have forgotten his exorbitant request, or he will have no choice but to welcome us back, given that he seems to be afraid to confront us in person. I would expect him at that juncture to display a bit of podsnappery (willfully ignore inconvenient facts)."

"Charles, you are indeed optimistic, and I cannot express enough gratitude that you are now here with me on this most trying adventure."

"It seems we have a plan!" he said.

AND SO WE decided we will leave tomorrow morning. I instructed my boys to arrive early, prepared for a collecting excursion that could last as long as a week.

7

APRIL 20, 1868

A GREAT MANY remarkable events have occurred since we departed from the village, such that it is difficult for me to believe it was merely three days past. But I shall attempt to tell of them in the order in which they occurred. First, I shall point out that, although I had my doubts during the first day and night of travel, I can now say with some confidence that I am rather well suited to a primitive existence in the tropical wilds. I have come to realize that nearly any difficulty can be overcome with some ingenuity and effort, and I have developed an increasing respect for the practical knowledge of Amborn and his patience in teaching me his apparently inherent skills. The other two boys, Miok and Loo, have proven themselves to be useful but do not seem to have much interest in learning to communicate with me or in teaching me, as Amborn does.

The first day of travelling was trying, as Charles and I were not yet accustomed to the rigors of moving great distances through untrodden forest. However, we soon developed a reasonable rhythm of walking and restful pausing that resulted in steady progress. My boys were considerably more burdened with supplies than Charles and I, but they seemed to travel without tiring, and I became determined to learn to match their pace.

I estimated that we travelled over four miles on the first day. We established our first camp without difficulty, and I was thankful we had practiced the procedures under less demanding circumstances next to my house. I can report with honesty that I slept reasonably well that night. Amborn had instructed me on how to construct a platform of sticks to elevate my sleeping mat several inches above the ground to limit the number of ants crawling over my body during the night. The boys were skillful in constructing these swiftly and with little apparent effort. I had brought a small supply of palm oil for my lamp and for applying to the supports to prevent the ants from climbing them, but Amborn showed me how to accomplish the same task with sap from a tree that he called *lanol*.

Travelling the second day became even more efficient, and by midday we had covered a distance equal to that of the entire previous day. In the afternoon, as we descended into a valley, my boys stopped and pointed at something. About fifty yards away, I saw movement in the dense trees and realized I was gazing upon the most magnificent bird I had ever seen. I knew it to be a cassowary, though I was sure these birds were not yet known to exist in this region of New Guinea. Its splendid blue and crimson head was held aloft at about the height of my chin by an absurdly slender neck. The bird slowly walked away from us, as if it held no fear of man. Charles saw it, too, and he took aim at it and shot, missing. My gun was loaded with eight shot, which at the considerable distance would have little effect. The bird fled into the forest and was not seen again. It was a disappointing loss, and Charles apologized profusely for failing to kill such a splendid specimen. My boys, apparently excited by the sighting, exchanged enthusiastic words. They then put down their loads and began constructing our camp.

A good number of daylight hours remained in which to travel, and I asked Amborn why we had stopped. He explained that the presence of the cassowary indicated we had arrived at our destination. This delighted me, not only because the journey had taken less time than I had presumed it would, but also because this meant that I might have further opportunities to shoot one of these remarkable birds.

I scouted the immediate area to confirm that fresh water could be procured nearby, and we set about establishing a camp that could sustain us for several days. When things were situated to my satisfaction, I gathered my three boys and attempted to explain that I wished for them to stay with us rather than returning to the village as Penapul had requested. I then gave them a length of fine calico and three new knives as a further incentive to stay. They responded to this by tearing the calico into three equal lengths so that they would each have their own, and then they compared their knives, pointing out the minutest differences that might indicate that their own was better than the other two. Amborn then explained, however, that they had no intention of leaving us alone. They did not remember or were perhaps unaware of the chief's request. This relieved my anxiety considerably. And again I was relieved, upon the first light of morning, to see that they had not snuck away during the night.

Our first full day of collecting was successful beyond my hopes, as I had become accustomed to my disappointing efforts nearer to Humboldt Bay. We saw two cassowaries, and

Charles succeeded in shooting one of them, which did much to ease his suffering personal esteem from the previous day's miss. This bird not only provided a most impressive skin and feathers, but also a substantial supply of meat that I found to have an agreeable flavor. I am inclined to write at length regarding the anatomical details of this bird, but that should wait until a later date when I have the time to compare specimens and adequately prepare manuscripts for publishing. In addition to the cassowary, we shot seven parrots of five species (including one of deep red), one cockatoo, two lories, three kingfishers, four pigeons of different species, four thrushes of the same species, three species of warblers, one sunbird, two cuckoos, fourteen flycatchers, and a honeysucker. With regard to mammals, we shot a small flying opossum and an opossum-like cuscus.

Insects, particularly butterflies and longicorn beetles, many with a brilliant metallic luster, appeared to be abundant. I collected the most impressive of those we saw, but I decided to devote a day to collecting more insects after first procuring a good representation of the area's birds and other animals.

And now, at the twilight of our second day of collecting, I will attempt to describe, with as much judicious thought as I can muster, the rather bewildering events of this day. If you have read these words from the beginning, I hope that you have by this point determined that I am a man of reasonable education and civilized notions, devoted to pursuing knowledge and advancing science. I am seldom prone to fantastical ideas or the superstitions inherent in those of a lower state of civilization. Please be mindful of this as you read the following words, as my only intent is to put to paper the things I have witnessed and my attempts to make sense of them.

Knowing that we had supplies for no more than four days of collecting, I began our second day determined to venture inland to the south from our base camp. Then on our third day, I reasoned, we would venture as far as possible to the east, and on our fourth day to the west. Hence we set out early. I had my boys bring choppers and instructed them to clear a wide path as we made our way south. My plan was to establish paths in each direction from our base camp so that we could return here on future collecting trips and use the same paths, thus reducing duplicated efforts. Based upon our success on the previous day, I was even considering building a permanent house at the site of our base camp.

Our progress south was slow, as the jungle was thick and required much chopping. At times, Charles and I even shouldered our guns and assisted with the work. By the time we had progressed about a mile, we had shot a reasonable collection of birds, including two species of parrots I had not collected before and a new pigeon. We had not seen any mammals, probably due to the excessive noise of our chopping efforts. However, suddenly I turned around to see that a large rat-like creature had approached us on the path we had just chopped. The animal had a hairless tail and long, pointed snout, and I recognized it as a bandicoot, although an unusually large type. Bandicoots are ground-dwelling marsupials, and several species have been found on islands of the Malay Archipelago, but none were known to occur in this part of New Guinea, so it was almost certainly a new species. I knew other species of bandicoots to be smaller than this, perhaps twelve inches from snout to base of the tail, but this one appeared to be twice that length. Most unusual was that it seemed to hold no fear of man, and it approached without hesitation. Thinking that perhaps it had simply not seen us, I told Charles to shoot it before it discovered its mistake and ran away. It was an easy shot and a clean kill.

I instructed my boy Miok to stay there and skin the bandicoot, as the entire carcass would be a burden to carry. He was to finish the task and then catch up to us as we continued to the south. But before we were even out of sight of Miok, another bandicoot of the same type approached us. By this time I was quite curious and told Charles to refrain from shooting. Again I thought the creature must have failed to see us, perhaps due to poor eyesight. Or perhaps it was remarkably stupid. The wretched creature approached us until it was merely a few feet away. It then stopped and settled on its belly upon the ground, as if it were too tired to go any farther. I nudged it with my boot and it did nothing more than shift its position a few inches.

I was completely confounded by this strange behavior, as was Charles, and it seemed to drive Amborn and Loo into a state of agitation. They talked with excitement to each other, ignoring Charles and myself as if they had forgotten we were there. I inquired to Amborn as to his opinion on the matter, and he talked to me so rapidly that I could understand none of his words. With some perseverance, I was able to calm him enough to communicate effectively. Apparently he and Loo had heard stories from other members of his tribe of such strange animals living in this place, but they had not had the opportunity to see them with their own eyes. This made me curious, so I inquired as to what other stories about this place they might have been told. Amborn discussed this briefly with Loo and they actually laughed together before he returned his attention to me. He explained that others of his tribe feared this place. Some had apparently travelled here to hunt and had not returned. But he made it clear that he and Loo did not hold the same fears, and I realized that these young men were, in this respect, similar to the boys of Europe. They were skeptical of the opinions of the older generation. Perhaps this is a universal characteristic of young men of all cultures.

Nevertheless, this new information caused me to again consider Penapul's motives for sending us to such a place. I hadn't long to contemplate such matters, however, because from the corner of my eye I detected yet another creature moving about. I looked at the spot and saw what appeared to be a tree kangaroo, although at that moment it was on the ground. Instead of foolishly approaching as the two bandicoots had done, this creature sat upon its haunches and carefully watched us. Having never seen a tree kangaroo, except in illustrations, I was quite anxious to add it to my collection. I attempted to direct Charles' attention to where I had seen it, so that he might shoot it, but by the time he had turned around it had disappeared among the thickest vegetation. We walked to the spot and looked about, but the creature was not to be found.

And then, as if this place were determined to confound us even more, a most alarming thing happened. Amborn crouched low to the ground and gesticulated for us to do the same. He pointed and said the word, *abokhai*, which I knew to mean "man" or "hunter." Charles and I looked to where he pointed, but we saw nothing. I was somewhat skeptical, as we had seen no signs of a village or any human presence at all in the region. Unlike the area near Amborn's village, there were no footpaths, stumps of chopped trees, territory markings, or any other indications that people existed here. After a minute or so Amborn must have decided the abokhai was gone, because he rose to his feet and proceeded to describe the man, using his hands to draw upon his own body various ornamentations the man had worn. He used his word for "green parrot" to indicate the type of feathers the man wore upon his head.

Notwithstanding Amborn's agitated state and his tribe's inclination to fantastical beliefs, I considered the possibility that he had indeed seen a man there. Amborn had usually been reliable regarding most matters. Perhaps it was merely a hunter from another tribe, who upon seeing us decided to avoid conflict or perhaps was frightened by the strange occurrence of two white men.

I decided we should continue moving south as we had planned, and we had made another half mile of progress with no incident of any interest occurring, when Miok finally caught up to us. As I turned to watch him approach, I saw that not only had he failed to bring with him his sack of supplies and collected specimens, but he also did not have the skin of the bandicoot. His hands were red from the bandicoot's blood, but all he carried with him was his skinning knife in one hand and his chopper in the other. Miok was in a state of agitation, and he claimed to have seen not only one, but three abokhai, or hunters. Apparently, two of them had been watching him when he saw them, and he had called out a greeting to them, but they had not responded. He then had seen a third abokhai watching from the opposite direction, upon which he abandoned his supplies and the bandicoot and ran to find us.

Unwilling to leave the specimens and supplies to be stolen by these hunters, if indeed they did exist, I decided we should return as a group to fetch them. I had little fear of being attacked by these strangers, as Amborn, Charles, and myself each carried a loaded gun.

As I now reflect on the events that happened next, they are confusing at best, and at worst they signify that my senses have possibly been attacked and made unreliable due to some spoiled food or intoxicating substance I may have recently swallowed. But I feel no other ill effects, and Charles assures me that he has seen and experienced the very same events. So I wish to write them down while my memory of them is fresh, and perhaps later as I review them with diligence and rigor, I may determine them to be mere symptoms of our exhaustion, dehydration, or some other condition.

As a group armed with three rifles, we returned to the place where Miok had stopped to skin the bandicoot. However, finding the exact location was not as easy as expected. It seemed we had not chopped the vegetation as low as I had thought, and finding the spot required some searching. When we eventually found it, the bandicoot carcass and skin were missing, with only a bloody area to show where they had lain upon the ground. However, it was Miok's sack of specimens and supplies that I found to be most mystifying. The bag was there on the ground, but its outermost edges seemed to have disintegrated, having been transformed into small dark particles resembling soil. The portion of the bag in the center appeared to be intact, but there was a ring of this soil-like substance about the outer edges, as if the bag were decaying and returning to its basic elements of nature on an unnatural schedule rapid beyond all reason.

I asked Charles to describe in his own words what he was witnessing, and this corroborated my own observations. Even as we stood and watched, this unnatural process of decay continued before our eyes, until the entire sack and its contents were no more than a pile of brown matter upon the ground, even giving off a smell that could not be mistaken for any other than that of moist, fertile soil.

My boys seemed as mystified by this sight as Charles and I

were, and they became quiet, whispering soft words between them that I could not discern. It was then that I saw one of the strange hunters with my own eyes. Although the man was partly concealed by a tree, he was near, and I saw that his appearance was quite striking, with handsome, well-defined physiognomy and clear skin that showed no signs of nutritional distress, scars, or disease. Numerous green parrot feathers were fastened to his hair, protruding upward in various directions, and there was pale face paint around the area of his eyes, looking somewhat like a mask. He wore little ornamentation or clothing, other than a cylindrical gourd fitted upon his sexual organ, shorter than those worn by the men of the Humboldt Bay tribe. One of his hands gripped a spear made of wood, its sharpened tip darkened from hardening over a fire. For a moment I gazed at him, and he at me, as I attempted to discern whether he was simply a product of my imagination. Just as I had acquired my wits enough to inform Charles of the man's presence, the native retreated and seemed to disappear into the vegetation surrounding him. I continued to gaze upon the spot, but he did not reappear.

I was then forced to admit that indeed we were being followed and observed by natives, and as we had all been distressed by what we had witnessed and had lost some of our supplies, I decided it best to return to our camp for the day. The strange and shy natives would hopefully be gone from the area by the next morning when we would return to continue collecting on our southward trail.

However, that was not the last confounding event, as we soon realized the path we had chopped with much effort was not as clear as I remembered it to be. In fact, we soon found ourselves searching for any sign of the path at all, as if we had become lost, or as if the path had never existed. I then found evidence of our chopping, in the form of a plant stem that had been severed, but it appeared that lateral branches lower on the stem had grown upward, so that the remaining plant was now just as tall as it had been before it was chopped. The result of this was that the path was no longer discernable. I found other similar chopped plants that had grown tall again, but these required considerable effort to locate, making it impossible to follow the path in such a way. Hence we were forced to find our way back to our camp without the benefit of a path. This took some time and was slowed by the fact that earlier we had not taken note of landmarks, assuming we would have no need for them.

My native boys have a heightened directional sense, though, allowing them to travel dense jungle better than European men could, and we found our camp before darkness set in, bringing great relief to my mind.

As my boys prepared a meal, I discussed with Charles the events of the day in an attempt to elucidate any overlooked details, and perhaps to find comfort in the rigor of analysis.

———

NOTE: Again I have included this conversation exactly as it took place, to help readers understand the decisions that were made leading up to subsequent fateful events.

———

"PERHAPS," said I, "it would be helpful if we were to separate each of the puzzling sights we have seen into their rightful categories. The appearance of the strange hunters, for example, may be entirely unrelated to our becoming lost, or to the unnatural transformation of Miok's sack of supplies into soil. Cause and effect should not be assumed without compelling evidence."

"Correct," said Charles. "We should consider only the facts as we have observed them. All else is lather and prunella (flimsy). Let us first consider this native you saw. I believe you said he had a rather strange appearance."

"Yes, although putting it to words may be cumbersome." I thought on this for a moment. "I am compelled to say that he seemed, well, out of place here. There was something about his appearance that set him apart from the Papuan natives I have seen thus far. A primitive and barbarous life here, existing naked and unwashed in the wildest jungle, results in a characteristic appearance that, until now, I believed to be without exception." I waved my hand at my boys. "Consider Amborn's tribe. They live in a place where they have access by trade to items from more civilized places, and yet even the younger boys and girls show the telltale signs of weathering, injury, privations, and disease. I imagine most of them cannot expect to live beyond thirty or forty years at most. But this man I saw, this hunter—it was as if I were looking upon the face and skin of a young boy, but he was a man, with a man's eyes. He gazed upon me with a look that I find hard to describe. His eyes held no fear, only curiosity, as if he were seeing something remarkable he had not seen before, in the same way I might have looked upon the tree kangaroo I saw today."

For some seconds Charles looked at me before speaking. "I wish I had seen the man myself," he said. "I imagine he was simply a young hunter who had never had the occasion of seeing white men before. This explanation would comfort me in its unassuming simplicity."

"For now I will accept that," I said with some uncertainty.

"I can't imagine that they have any cause for obstinacy," Charles said. "Should it please the pigs (if God is willing), these natives may even be willing to assist us in our endeavor. I hope that they approach us so that I might see them with my own eyes."

"We will know soon enough," said I. "Let us next consider the chopped plants growing to their original height in a matter of mere hours. I suggest that we assume this phenomenon, rather than being attributed to botanical tissue growth, which seems impossible at the rate we witnessed, to instead be a result of a tropism."

"A tropism?"

"Yes, yes. My friend, Mr. Wallace, has discussed tropisms, as they are of particular interest to Charles Darwin. The word refers to a tendency of some plants to move toward or away from a stimulus, such as sunlight. Some plants can change their position and angle by expanding the cells on one side of the stem, thus bending toward the sun much more quickly than could be possible with normal growth. And it is possible that some plants might respond thus to trauma."

"Such as being chopped with a blade," said Charles.

"Precisely. I have heard this theory referred to as traumatropism, and it may explain how the lower stems of the plants we chopped were able to compensate in such a way, perhaps expanding the cells on the bottom side of each stem, causing them to bend upward."

Charles appeared to be unconvinced of this, but he said, "So we have adequately—or perhaps I should say tolerably—explained the native hunters and the chopped vegetation. And the unenergetic behavior of the bandicoots can be explained in many ways, such as disease or the fearlessness of being unaware of the threat of man. But what possible hypothesis can we batter through to explain a sack decomposing before our eyes?"

We contemplated this in silence for some minutes.

"The tropical climate holds many mysteries yet unsolved," said I. "The atmosphere here is quite warm and pure. Perhaps this, as well as some fertile or abounding characteristic of the soil, results in unusually industrious organisms of putrefaction."

Charles nodded slightly while frowning, indicating his doubts. "Or perhaps the elusive native you saw is in some way responsible. Perhaps he applied some softening ointment or poultice that his tribe may use to hasten decay." His doubtful frown remained.

Finally I sighed in defeat. "I have seen nothing like it before, and my thoughts fail me. Perhaps a decent night of sleep and the light of a new day will renew our perspective on this. Perhaps tomorrow, Charles, the answer will find us."

"Or perhaps," said he, "we will find that we have been allured by the blue roses of an impossible conundrum."

THAT IS an account of today's events. Even at this late hour, as I sit upon my primitive bed, writing by the light of my palm oil lamp and contemplating a plan for tomorrow, I have little confidence in our explanations for what we have witnessed. My curiosity implores me to set out to the south again, perhaps marking our passage rather than chopping a path, so that we can further investigate any secrets this strange place may yield.

8

APRIL 21, 1868

IT SEEMS ALMOST certain these words will be my last, as I have little hope of waking to see another day once I close my eyes to sleep. Furthermore, it is equally probable that these words will never be read. If by some miraculous turn of fate they are found and read by civilized eyes, they may be dismissed as the rantings of a dying man. If you do find yourself in possession of this notebook, please know that I, Samuel Thaddeus Inwood, English gentleman and man of science, am truly sorry for the pain of bereavement forced upon my parents, my betrothed, the family of my assistant Charles Newman, and the families of my boys Amborn, Miok, and Loo. Perhaps most importantly, please know that here, in this darkest jungle, there remains hidden a most mysterious phenomenon. It is a substance of no great beauty or magnificence. But this is misleading, because at the least it holds the most peculiar properties, and at most it may be the humble disguise of God Himself.

I must get on with it, lest I pass away before explaining.

Following yesterday's strange events, we determined early

this morning to try again to travel south from our base camp to continue collecting. I tore some calico into strips and tied these to trees to mark our way.

After an hour of travelling to the south, during which we had shot several new birds, I saw a tree kangaroo in the branches above us. It gazed upon me in such a way as to make me think it may have been the very same tree kangaroo I had seen the previous day. It had the same look in its eyes—curious but not afraid. This time the creature made no attempt to run away, and I pointed it out to Charles, who always kept his gun loaded with a ball. Charles took aim and shot, and the tree kangaroo fell to the ground. We approached it, and to all appearances it was dead.

Just as I congratulated Charles on an excellent shot, I heard a disturbance in the trees behind us, followed by a snorting sound from Charles I had never heard him make before. I turned to him, and to my horror saw that he had been run through from behind by a native's spear. With a wretched expression upon his face, he groped at the bloody point of the spear protruding from his abdomen. I desperately tried cocking the hammer on my gun, but it slipped from my thumb, and my number eight shot fired uselessly into the ground. The owner of the spear pulled it free. Charles staggered and turned to face his attacker. The native immediately ran him through again, this time through the throat. Charles fell to the ground, twisting wildly about, struggling to breathe but inhaling only his own blood.

Amborn, Miok, and Loo dropped their sacks of supplies and the gun and began running back the way we had come. This turned out to be the worst direction possible, as two more natives stepped forth from the trees, directly in their path. My boys pulled their skinning knives from their waist cords, however these were pitiable weapons against the attackers' long spears. Amborn let out a dismal shriek, attempting to sound fierce, but his voice carried the tenor of desperate fear.

The man who had stabbed Charles appraised me for a moment, looking in particular at my gun, which was still smoking from the ineffectual shot. He must have decided that I presented no further threat, as he moved away from me and into position behind my boys, preventing their retreat. Before I had the wits or means to protect them, the boys were savagely attacked by all three of the men, pierced repeatedly in their heads and necks until they lay dead upon the ground.

In a state of bewilderment I turned my eyes from the bodies of my boys back to Charles, who was at this point hardly moving at all, his eyes wide and staring directly at me. I had been trying uselessly to reload my gun, and I simply tossed it aside and knelt beside Charles. The natives were coming for me, and I decided my last moment would be better spent consoling my dear friend. I put my hand upon his cheek and realized I was too late, as Charles was already dead.

I heard the murderous savages speak to each other as they stood behind me. Still on my knees, I turned to them and held out my hands, determined on appearing agreeable. But instead of looking at me, their attention was fixed upon something to the side. I turned to look, and there was the tree kangaroo I had instructed Charles to shoot. I had been quite sure the rifle ball had killed it, but obviously I had been mistaken, for now the creature was sitting up, licking its substantial wound.

The resurrected creature then walked toward us until it was directly between me and the men who intended to murder me. What happened next you might find difficult to believe, but as these are likely my last words, I have every intention of writing what I know to be true, other opinions be damned. The tree kangaroo sat upon its haunches and moved its forepaws about in a most peculiar way, looking very much as if the gesticulations held some intelligent meaning rather than the brutish and random movements of a lower animal. The Papuan men watched this display with interest, after which they exchanged words I could not understand, as they had little resemblance to the language of Penapul's tribe.

As they talked, shook their heads, and pointed in my direction, I waited, distressed and stupefied, for my death. One of them was the same man I had seen the day before, with green parrot feathers still protruding from his frizzly hair. The other two wore woven bands around their arms with black cassowary feathers attached, but they had no head-dresses or feathers upon their heads. All of them bore the same strange appearance of having bodies of men wrapped in the youthful skin of boys.

At last they seemed to come to an agreement about some-thing and turned their attention to me. I tried to prepare for my death by expressing a silent prayer, but my thoughts were jumbled and quite useless. Instead of immediately murdering me as I expected them to, they took hold of my shirt and tore it from my body. After passing my ruined shirt between them and observing it with curiosity, they tossed it to the ground. They grasped my boots and pulled on them, causing me to tumble. They pulled my boots from my feet, inspected them, and tossed them next to the shirt. When they came for my trousers, I tried to resist. One of them clubbed me on the side of my face with the shaft of his spear, nearly knocking me senseless. They removed the last of my clothing, leaving me in a state of nature, without dignity. The brute with green feathers upon his head picked up my spectacles, which had been knocked to the ground. He inspected them for a moment then picked up my satchel, which had been pulled from me when my shirt had been taken. He removed my field note-book, looked it over, and returned it to the satchel along with my spectacles. He then placed the satchel over his shoulder as he had seen it on mine, which resulted in laughter from his companions.

With blurred vision due to my spectacles having been stolen and the blood flowing from my forehead into my eyes, I watched one of the men select a sapling about an inch in diameter and pull it from the soil. He removed the lateral stems and leaves until it was no more than a flexible stick with a point at one end and a soil-covered root ball at the other. He and the others approached me, and I rose to my knees so that I might hold my head upright with some small amount of dignity before being run through with their spears.

As the savage with green feathers gazed at me, I said, "If you wish to kill me, have the decency to do it now."

The man actually smiled, although this hardly provided me any comfort. His companions held my arms and head so that I could not struggle. With one hand, the green-feathered man then grasped the pectoral muscle on one side of my chest and pulled it outward. With his other hand he drove the point of his spear entirely through the pinched fold of muscle. I cried out in despair but was unable to move. He withdrew the spear and then threaded the tip of the sapling through the bleeding hole until he could grasp the tip as it came out the other side of the fold of flesh.

The piercing of the spear had been distressingly painful, but it hardly prepared me for the torment that ensued when the man held the distal tip of the sapling and pulled on it until the entire sapling had passed through my pectoral muscle and the wide root ball stopped it from being pulled through completely. I felt the glorious relief of fainting coming upon me, but the man then pulled on his end of the sapling, forcing me upward onto my feet in the most insufferable way.

I attempted to beg them to simply kill me, but coherent words would not form upon my lips. As I watched them through enfeebled eyes, one of the men opened a small leather pouch that hung from his neck. He scooped some unknown substance from the pouch onto his finger as if it were betel. Systematically and with apparent purpose, he smeared some of the substance upon the bodies of Charles and my three boys, and then upon the pile of my clothing and the three guns. While these puzzling acts took place, the tree kangaroo I had thought to be dead sat upon its haunches and watched, as a domestic dog might watch with interest its European owners preparing breakfast in the kitchen.

Without a word spoken, the natives turned to leave. The man with green feathers pulled on the sapling in such a way that I was forced to follow to avoid great pain. It was then that I realized the sapling was nothing more than a cruel leash with which to lead me and prevent me from running away.

For perhaps an hour I was pulled along, naked and bleeding, by my pectoral muscle, occasionally stumbling and causing myself great discomfort. My mind could think of nothing but putting one foot before the other, and of what barbarous plans these savages intended for me. If they were cannibals, it seemed odd that they had left behind the bodies of Charles and my boys. Alternatively, if they intended to keep me alive, it seemed they had failed at this, as I would surely perish from the wound they had inflicted upon me. Without proper medicines, which I felt sure they did not have, it would soon fester and ulcerate. So what possible purpose could they have for me?

We finally arrived at the indigenes' village, by which time I was significantly weakened from bleeding and exhaustion. I saw several huts, built some height above the ground and supported by corner poles as the huts were in Amborn's village. But I had little opportunity to observe further, as more tribesmen, perhaps ten in total, soon surrounded me. I saw no women among them. There was much talking among the men, revealing again that their language was unfamiliar to me. As I stood there I began to stagger on my feet, and when the native holding my rudimentary leash finally released it, I fell to my knees.

The talking soon stopped. It appeared that an agreement had been reached. Three of the men left and soon returned carrying a most ordinary looking object, which they set upon the ground in front of me. It appeared to be a large lump of clay, resting upon a platform of poles fastened together as a means of carrying it. I had no idea of the object's nature or purpose, but in my desperate state I could only imagine it would somehow be used to further maim or perhaps kill me. I staggered to my feet and attempted to run. Immediately I was subdued and held upon the ground.

What happened next is difficult for me to put to words, but as I have said, I have determined to describe all the details of my last hours, in case this notebook might somehow be found.

Held firmly to the ground, I watched as one of the savages brought forth a sharpened wedge of bamboo. He grasped my bare foot and pushed the foot down on its side. He then positioned the sharpened edge against the large tendon above my heel. The man next to him raised his foot and brought it down upon the bamboo wedge, forcing it to cut entirely through the tendon, severing it.

So shocked was I by the ruthless cruelty of this act that I hardly cried out in my suffering, simply watching as they performed the same operation on my other heel.

I was then unable to run, walk, or even stand upon my feet, and the men dragged me by my arms back to the lump of clay. They dropped me before it and then stood watching.

I crouched there upon my knees, sobbing. I had no idea what they wanted of me.

A spear point punctured my thigh, and then another, forcing me to crawl closer to the object. This continued mercilessly until I was merely inches from it. It appeared to be nothing more than clay, perhaps dug from the ground, pressed into a somewhat spherical lump about two feet in diameter. I could not imagine what sinister purpose it might serve in my prolonged and unpleasant death. Yet another spear to my thigh forced me upon it. I placed my hands on its surface, thinking the savages must wish for me to do something with it.

It may be assumed that what I remember happening next is the fevered and false visions of a dying man. However, even at this moment of my last twilight, it seems to me to have been real and true.

Upon laying my hands on the clay, I saw before my eyes a sight that I thought to be of my mind's trickery. I saw figures there, like letters of some unknown script, just before my face. I withdrew my hands, intending to rub the blood from my eyes, and the figures vanished. I blinked and looked up at my murderous captors. They watched me with great interest. I returned my hands to the clay and the symbols appeared again. Everything within my view was blurred due to my missing spectacles, but these figures were in perfect focus.

With one hand remaining on the clay, I waved my other hand through the apparition. Although I felt nothing against my skin, the strange figures moved about in reaction, as if they were made of wood and were floating about upon a pool of water. I held my hand to the side of one of them and then waved it through the figure. The figure flew to the side and disappeared, as if my hand had pushed it away. I repeated this operation with each of the other figures until they were all gone.

But soon after I had rid the last of them from my sight, the figures appeared before me again, perhaps fifteen of them. It occurred to me that I had perhaps gone completely mad. Seeking some measure of comfort, I withdrew from the clay, and the supernatural vision vanished. But this did not please the natives, and they stabbed at me viciously with their spears, forcing me to lay my hands upon it yet again. And again the figures appeared. But this time, soon after appearing, they began to move about on their own, with no influence from me. One figure moved to the side and stopped. Then two more moved out of the main group and stopped just above the first one, followed by three that stopped above those, and then four above those. There were still six more in the original group, and I watched, somewhat expecting to see five of them move into place above the last four, completing what appeared to be a numerical pattern. But they remained still, so I extended a hand and waved five of them into their logical place.

They all vanished before my eyes and were replaced by even more than there were before. Again the figures began moving, with one taking position on the bottom and two above it. But then, instead of three moving into place above the two, this time four of the figures moved into position above the two, and then eight more above the four. When they did not move again, I carefully waved sixteen figures into place above the eight.

They all vanished and were replaced by perhaps a hundred more. But suddenly I felt overcome with pain and confusion and fell to my side, releasing the mysterious lump of clay, again causing the figures to vanish. What manner of substance was this? Civilized man was the only creature capable of arranging such mathematical patterns. And how could these figures appear and move in such a way? It seemed as if I were being tested, to prove I was capable of under-standing the patterns. It then occurred to me, however, that I was a dying man, and my state of dying was precisely why these visions had befallen me. God Himself was speaking to me. He was testing me, determining whether I was worthy of entering His Kingdom.

I was torn from my forlorn thoughts by the point of a savage's spear. By this time my body was bleeding from numerous punctures, as well as my severed heel tendons, and I was feeling like I might lose consciousness. The natives forced me up to my knees and I again rested myself against the clay, this time in order to prevent my body from collapsing. The strange figures appeared before me yet again. I gazed upon them as they began to move into another pattern. I now felt oddly comforted, due to my belief that God was there with me. I simply watched the figures, with no intention of moving, waiting for my final moment to arrive.

The natives began talking behind me. They were becoming agitated. Still I did not move. Suddenly I was aware of extreme pain in my thigh. I looked down to see the sharp end of a spear, red with my own blood and protruding out by several inches. Then another appeared at its side, having been driven through my leg with great force. The pain of this caused me to abandon my attempts at dying with a measure of dignity. I wrapped my arms about the clay and held it tightly, hoping that His presence within it might ease my passing.

I cried out, "God, spare me! I can endure no more!"

A brief moment later there was an odd sensation of tingling within my hands. It quickly spread to my arms and then throughout my body. When the sensation passed into my legs, my pain diminished. I looked down at the spear tips, which were now being twisted about by the men in their attempts to force me to do whatever it was that they wished of me.

Suddenly, in my thigh burned a pain even greater than before. There was the smell of burning flesh. Before I could comprehend what was occurring, the spear tips ignited with flames. As I cried out in my suffering, the natives pulled their spears from my flesh and stared at the tips, which were still burning. They quickly recovered their senses and extinguished the spears upon the ground.

The events following this apparent miracle are difficult for me to recall, as I had been driven to a stupefied state. I fell to the ground, unable to support myself even with the help of God Himself. The natives stood over me as they engaged in a discussion. Finally, they grasped my ruined legs and dragged me some distance. One of them tied a rope around my ankles, with no regard for my wounds. I remember groaning at the pain this caused, as I had become too weak to cry out. Then, as they hoisted me up by my ankles to one of the raised houses, I discovered I was still quite capable of screaming.

The next thing I recall was awaking upon the floor of the hut. The native men were gone but for one, the savage with green feathers upon his head. He stood above me, gazing at me with no intelligent expression upon his face. When he saw me lift my head, he kicked one of my feet, which caused me to groan.

"What do you wish of me?" I said to him.

He continued to gaze at me for a moment, and then he spoke slowly and clearly.

"*Gu laléo. Gu aup Lamotelokhai.*"

NOTE: By the time I transcribed this notebook, I had a good grasp of the language of this tribe, and I determined that translating some of the conversations exactly as they took place would help readers understand important events. Below is my translation (added when transcribing this notebook):

"YOU ARE AN OUTSIDER. You talk to the Lamotelokhai."

HE THEN REMOVED MY SATCHEL, which was still hanging from his shoulder, and dropped it on the floor beside me. He went to the door and began descending the ladder. Before he was out of my sight, he glanced at me a final time and smiled, exposing perfectly healthy teeth.

After lying alone in the hut for some time, I crawled to the wall so that I might sit against it. I opened my satchel to find that all its contents were still there, including my spectacles, notebook, ink, pens, and nibs. I inspected the wounds on my heels. They had stopped bleeding, which surprised me, but I knew that even if I were to survive another day, I would likely never again be capable of walking.

So my fate, it seems, is determined. I shall perish here, if not tonight, then certainly within a few days. As poor Charles might have said, I am creating a vacancy, and I have no return ticket. I have spent the last hours of daylight writing an account of these events. I now feel overcome with the need for rest, and my fantastical determination that God has somehow spoken to me through a lump of clay seems more absurd with every passing moment.

9

NEVER HAVE I been a particularly religious man. I dare say that my relations with God have been primarily based upon necessity. I felt it necessary to attend my family's church, St Mary Aldermary. I felt it necessary to agree to be married to Lindsey, my betrothed, in the very same church. Many of my colleagues in science seem to delight in discoveries that most confound the doctrines of Christianity. I, however, as a matter of necessity, have sought to recognize the hand of God in every wonder of nature, as otherwise the complexities of the natural world bewilder my thoughts. Furthermore, upon those rare occasions when I have felt my very life to be at risk, I have prayed to God for the kindness of good fortune.

And so it is that I feel I have betrayed the graces that God has bestowed upon me, as even at this moment, when ample evidence suggests that God has spared my life, I cannot help but question if it was indeed His will. Now that immediate death no longer haunts my thoughts, I feel a need to look at my situation rationally and without preconception. What is it, exactly, that is happening to me? If rigorous analysis proves that my circumstances have improved due to the forgiving hand of God, then I shall forever be His grateful servant. However, if, as I am beginning to suspect, my condition is due simply to the influences of natural, corporeal phenomena, then I must endeavor to better understand these phenomena, as they surely are unknown to science and the civilized world.

I shall describe the events of this day to facilitate this analysis.

I awoke several times during the night. Surprisingly, this was due to reasons other than the pain of my injuries. The first time I awoke, it was due to experiencing a most unusual dream. It seemed to me at the time to be real, such that I awoke truly believing I had experienced its events. The dream began in the heavens, in which innumerable stars populated the dark night sky. However, rather than the familiar situation of stars overhead and ground below, there were stars in every direction—above, below, and to all sides. I was able to look in any direction at will but was unable to see my own body. There was nothing but black sky and stars. To my surprise I saw no familiar constellations. And I had considerable time to examine the stars, so long in fact that I was nearly overcome with a sense of aloneness, as if I had been there with only stars as my company for years, or perhaps centuries.

At last the previously unchanging view of the heavens began to shift, and I had the sensation that it was I who was moving. The stars began to shift faster, and faster still, until new stars were passing by me before I could get a proper look at them. If there were constellations that I knew, they passed by unrecognized. Again, this state of movement seemed to go on for a very long time, and my sense of aloneness intensified.

Finally, a star in the distance seemed to grow larger, as if it were getting gradually closer. As it continued to grow, it became so bright that I could not gaze directly upon it, and it was then that I saw something quite astonishing. Beside the star was a world, steadily growing larger as I drew nearer to it. It was rather like looking at the moon when it is full and round, but instead of a stark and dead surface, this world was vivid with blue oceans, brown continents, and white clouds. As the world drew even closer, I saw something else. It was a smaller world, the moon with which we are all familiar. I knew then that I was gazing upon the earth itself, in a way that no man had ever done before. Although I knew it must have been the earth, the shapes and arrangements of the continents puzzled me, as they did not resemble those that modern man has determined to be so, as shown on every globe installed in schools of civilized countries. The continents before me were somewhat recognizable, but arranged in such a way that reminded me of a map I had seen, created by the geographer Antonio Snider-Pelligrini, in which he theorized that the continents had gradually drifted about on the earth's surface. If Mr. Snider-Pellegrini was correct, I was observing the earth as it appeared in some long-past age.

The earth grew larger and filled my entire vision, and still I moved closer, until I passed directly through a thin layer of clouds. In the next instant I was on a barren, brown landscape, devoid of any discernible living things. Bare rocks and volcanic mountains could be seen in every direction to the horizon. Again I had the strange sensation that an unimaginable duration of time was passing, and as I watched, the landscape around me began to change. Bodies of water advanced and receded in a matter of seconds. Brown rocks and dirt gave way to a thin layer of green upon the ground, followed by taller vegetation. Great forests filled the landscape, and like the bodies of water, they advanced and receded again and again. Mountains rose abruptly and gradually leveled out as they were washed into the seas. Still I felt a sense of aloneness, but now this was alleviated by another sensation, that of great anticipation.

At last the passing of time diminished. I found myself in a jungle, not unlike the forest of my present situation. The smell of moist soil entered my nostrils, and I heard the singing of birds and felt the tropical climate. To my surprise, upon the ground before me was a tree kangaroo, of the same type Charles had shot. It gazed at me, and then it turned and ran away. I followed. The creature led me directly to the village of the barbarous indigenes who had killed Charles and my boys, and there upon its carrying frame was the same confounding lump of clay. But this time, in this strange and vivid dream, I did not give a moment's thought to the presence of God. Instead, I was overcome with a different understanding, that there was indeed a presence there, but most assuredly not that of God. Notwithstanding that an intelligent presence within a lump of clay naturally implies an act of God, I somehow was aware that this presence, rather than being the creator of this earth, was upon the earth after having journeyed a great distance.

That is when I awoke. And rather than lying in the darkness and brooding over my ruined body and impending death, I thought only of the importance of my dream. Had it been more than a mere dream?

I awoke again later in the night, thinking that ants or some other pests were creeping about upon my body and entering my wounds. It felt as if each puncture and gash were crawling with activity. But when I felt them with my fingertips, I could find no evidence of marauding insects, and I had no source of light for a visual inspection. As I lay there trying to rest, I continued to feel as if things were moving about on my wounds, or perhaps that the torn skin itself were moving.

Eventually I awoke yet again and saw that the night had passed and so had much of the morning. I heard the softly spoken words of my Papuan captors somewhere outside. As I lay there on my side, gazing at the hut's wall and slowly gaining my senses, I realized that I felt no pain. I sat up, surprisingly with no discomfort. Still completely naked, I inspected my wounds, upon which I became greatly confused. The spear punctures were nearly healed, as was my pectoral muscle that had been run completely through. Fresh and pale skin had grown over them, making them appear as scars from injuries that had occurred weeks before. Was it possible that I had slept for such a long time? I rubbed the scars with my fingers and still felt no pain. Next I inspected my severed heel tendons and found them to be in the same advanced state of healing. I knew this to be quite impossible, as severed heel tendons snap apart in such a way that they must be forcibly pulled together to be carefully sewn, an operation that rarely results in a patient's ability to walk or run as he once did. But my tendons seemed to have reattached themselves. I put pressure upon one heel and the tendon grew tight without rupturing. I then rose to my feet and carefully took a few steps. To my amazement, the tendons functioned satisfactorily. I walked to the door of the hut, which was about fifteen feet above the ground, and below me two tribesmen sat together, quietly talking. When they saw me, one of them stood and shouted, at the same time thrusting his spear in my direction, a clear message that I was not to leave the hut. And so I spent the next few hours pacing, contemplating my miraculous recovery, and feeling my body seemingly grow stronger with each passing moment.

Finally, I sat with my satchel to write these events in my notebook.

To any civilized person who might be reading these words, you probably assume that there can be only two possible explanations: either I have gone mad, or God did indeed act on my behalf. I did, after all, beg for His mercy while being tormented. However, now that my mind is clear, I can assure you that there is yet a third possibility, that the mysterious lump of clay, which is not a vessel of God after all, is the author of my current existence. It is a most extraordinary entity, and if I continue to grow stronger and can avoid being murdered by the savages holding me captive, I intend to learn what I can of its particulars.

10

APRIL 23, 1868

LITTLE ELSE OF importance happened yesterday after I had written in my notebook, although my captors did finally bring food and water. Late in the afternoon, two tribesmen climbed to my hut and gave me a hollowed-out gourd filled with sago paste, and another containing dirty brown water. I was much in need of these and readily accepted them. Sitting naked upon the floor, I devoured them as my captors watched. One of the men was the savage with green parrot feathers in his hair, the very man who had killed Charles. The other was a man I had not seen before. White cockatoo feathers protruded from his frizzly hair in the same fashion as the green feathers of the first man. In addition, the man with white feathers wore more ornamentation than any of the other tribesmen I had so far seen. Bands of woven grass encircled his upper arms, adorned with black cassowary feathers, and a broad necklace of small white and orange cowrie mollusk shells hung about his neck. This was so wide that it covered his shoulders and much of his chest. Like the other men, he wore a hollow gourd upon his sexual organ, and I saw that his gourd was adorned with figures carved into its surface. Something seemed familiar about these figures, and then I recognized some of them as the same figures that had appeared in my vision when I had put my hands to the mysterious lump of clay. I pointed to the figures on the gourd and asked what significance they held, but of course the men could not understand my words.

At that moment I realized my thoughts had transcended mere concerns over my immediate death. I knew then, and I still believe now, that I may die at the hands of these savages, but a great scientific curiosity was arising within me. I had encountered a phenomenon I could not explain, one that could be of great importance to science. Rather than thinking only of my escape, I began to have thoughts on how I might convince the natives to allow me to live so that I could learn more about what I had observed the last few days. And I was encouraged in this respect when the two men approached me, pointed at the various wounds they had inflicted upon me, and exchanged words. They were discussing my remarkable recovery, indicating that it was important to them.

"Samuel," I said to them, and I placed my hand on my chest. They gazed at me for a moment, and then I stated my name again.

To my surprise, they each repeated my name, although the pronunciation was less than perfect. I pointed to them and then used gesticulations I thought might express my desire to know their names.

Apparently this worked, as the man with green feathers placed his hand upon his own chest and said, "Sinanie."

"Sinanie," I said back to him.

Then the man with white feathers touched his chest and said, "Matiinuo."

"Matiinuo," said I.

The two men gazed at me a moment longer, then they left me alone with nothing to do but ponder my fate.

My second night as a prisoner in the hut was more restful. I slept with relatively little concern or discomfort, notwithstanding the fact that I had no proper bed. Before sleeping I had to relieve my bowels, after which I kicked the feces out the door. Upon doing this, I saw that there were no natives below to prevent my escape. I considered this option for some minutes and even jumped about frantically in the hut to see if my injured ankles were healed to the point of allowing me to run. But the results of this were of mixed implications. On the one hand I experienced no pain and felt as if I could outrun the swiftest native. On the other hand the very truth of this inclined me to believe that, should I success-fully escape, I would never have the opportunity to under-stand what manner of substance could have such astounding qualities of healing. I would be leaving behind a most signifi-cant discovery.

It also occurred to me that, should I escape and somehow find my way back to the Humboldt Bay village, I would hardly be welcome there once it was known that Amborn, Miok, and Loo had been murdered while in my service. It seemed that my safety there might be as uncertain as it was here. And so, as astounding as it might seem, I chose to stay in my present situation.

I awoke this morning to another surprise. Unlike the previous night, I had slept without dreaming. Upon awaking, however, I was comforted by a most uncharacteristic sense of well-being. As I lay naked upon the floor, marveling at how I could feel so fit, I attempted to recall the multitude of injuries I had suffered. To my amazement, visions of each event I endeavored to remember came to me with perfect clarity. I could relive each moment as if it were happening all over again. This was at the same time interesting and alarming. I arose and paced about the hut, thinking of events from my past. Each of them, no matter how small or unimportant, appeared as a perfectly detailed vision in my mind. I was able to recall things I had long forgotten: words spoken or read, acquaintances met, and sights I had seen years before, even well back into my youth. It was all quite astounding, and I amused myself in such a way for much of the day, fearing that this unusual intellectual ability might expire at any moment.

As if this were not astonishing enough, there was yet another surprise. As I paced about the hut, it occurred to me that everything before my eyes was perfectly focused, despite the fact that my spectacles were still in my satchel, where I had placed them the previous night. Not since I was merely a boy had my unaided eyes seen things with such clarity. Hence, my spectacles remained in the satchel, as I apparently had no further need for them.

Later in the afternoon, Sinanie and Matiinuo climbed up to my hut again. When I saw that they had no weapons, but instead had brought only food and water, I exclaimed to them with excitement the details of my newfound ability. Of course they could understand none of it, and they observed me in silence for some time. They placed gourds of water and sago paste on the floor, and then Matiinuo came forward. He opened one of his hands, and in it was a white cockatoo feather, similar to those attached to his hair. He grasped the feather with two fingers and then held it against his hair. After a brief moment he moved it to another spot upon his hair, and then to another after that, as if he were unsure of where it should be attached.

I gazed at his frizzly hair, and then I knew. I extended my

hand and actually touched a spot on his head. "It was there," said I. "Yesterday the feather was in that exact location."

He looked at Sinanie and said, *"Mülalüp nokhu-khata-pa amo-ba-lé. Khakhul-fekho lép-telo. Imoné-fekho khil gam."*

Sinanie said, *"Yu sol nggulun?"*

Matiinuo then said, *"Nokhu be-khelép-telo-n-din-da. Nokhu ülmo belén bakha-li. Nokhu funép ülmo lulo-kha-lé. Nokhu funép nggawél ülmo."*

NOTE: Again, I have determined that translating some of the conversations exactly as they took place will help readers understand important events. On that day, of course, I could not understand the natives' words. Now, however, as I transcribe this notebook, I am able to provide a translation:

MATIINUO: "We have done things like that in former times. Yesterday he was ill. Now he is healthy and improved."

Sinanie: "Is he a new teacher?"

Matiinuo: "We cannot know. We will not kill him on this day. Perhaps we will kill him tomorrow or the day after. Perhaps we are not willing to kill him."

AFTER THIS EXCHANGE OF WORDS, the two men gazed at me for a moment, and then they descended to the ground, leaving me alone yet again.

As the afternoon now turns to evening, there is little for

me to do other than employ my newfound mental capacity to recall every detail of what I have already learned about these unusual natives and the lump of clay they keep concealed here. Perhaps tomorrow I will have the opportunity to learn more.

11

APRIL 24, 1868

I T IS a rare thing for a man to experience an event that transforms his mind such that he then views the world with an entirely new perspective. Most men may experience only one such event, perhaps as they pass from boy to man and discover for the first time that all people are capable of malicious and deceitful acts, or perhaps when they learn that they are to be forever subject to a flourishing attraction to members of the fair sex. Nonetheless, in the single day that has passed since I last wrote, I have experienced not one, but two such events, and I fear I shall never be the same man that I was.

I will begin with my dream of last night, my third night as a prisoner here. I hesitate to use the word *dream* to describe it, as this word implies an unimportant, often senseless transmogrification of a person's thoughts, somehow conjured during one's sleep. But this dream, like the dream of my first night here, had little resemblance to any dreams of my past. It was clear and detailed in such a way as to indicate to me that the vision was not from my own imagination, but rather was being shown to me. I am sure of this, because the contents of the vision were quite beyond my own mind's capacity to concoct.

At some time during the night, which I believe to have been the early morning just before awaking, I was suddenly alert and quite aware of my surroundings. But on this occasion, instead of finding myself in the heavens with nothing but stars to see, I was perhaps twenty feet above the ground, in some strange land unlike any I have seen in my travels. There were rocks below me, and among the rocks were pools of water, rippling from the actions of fish or other aquatic creatures just below the surface. The pools of water stretched out into the distance as far as I could see. Most unusual, however, was the odd red hue of the entire scene, due to the sun just rising from the horizon. And never had I seen a sun like this. It seemed to be far larger than I had ever seen the sun, even just at sunrise, and its color was a deep and spellbinding red. As I watched the sun rise higher, it did not turn from red to brilliant yellow as I have always known the sun to do. Instead, it remained red, although it became much brighter, and it cast a beautiful pink light upon the landscape.

As I watched this immense, crimson sun rising, I noticed yet another curious thing—a web of thin threads suspended in the sky somewhere between the sun and myself. These threads were clearly visible against the red sun, and when I looked elsewhere in the sky I saw that they were faintly visible from one horizon to the other, as if the entire world were trapped in the vast web of a spider.

I had little time to ponder the impossibility of such a notion, for I began moving, flying perhaps ten yards above the ground. The swirling pools of water passed by below me, gradually at first, but then I flew faster and faster until they passed by in a bewildering blur. I looked ahead, and in the distance I saw a thin, pale line that stretched from the ground all the way up to the heavens. I was sure this was a portion of the vast web that filled the sky far above me, somehow connecting it to the ground. The pale line grew in size as I flew closer to it, until what I had thought was a thin vertical line turned out to be an immense white, cylindrical tower several miles in diameter. I had never dreamed that such a structure could be built and could not imagine what it was that prevented the tower from collapsing under its own weight and falling to the earth. And to my bewilderment, there were other such towers visible in every direction, so far away that they appeared as long threads stretching straight up until they vanished into the heavens.

Before I had time to fully appraise the vastness of the tower before me, I flew into a wide corridor leading to its interior. This corridor bustled with activity, and at first I thought it was filled with people, walking to and fro on their daily business, as crowded as Oxford Street in London. However, I soon determined that they were not people at all, but rather some type of creature that walked with a very different posture. They carried themselves in a nearly horizontal state, with two legs at the posterior and one much thinner leg near the anterior end, which seemed to stiffen with each step and support the creature's entire weight as the two rear legs swung forward, thus making progress as if using a crutch. I could discern little else regarding their anatomical structure, as I passed by them too swiftly, but it was clear they were unlike any creatures I had ever seen. This was quite bewildering to me, particularly when considering the fact that they moved about with apparent intelligent purpose.

I found the corridor itself to be of interest, as the walls were of a peculiar white material that seemed to emit its own light, thus illuminating the entire hall in a most pleasing way. I continued moving through the long corridor toward the tower's interior, but I saw that it was joined to many lateral corridors, all of them brimming over with the strange creatures walking with purpose to unknown destinations.

Just when I began to think the corridor might lead me entirely through the tower to the opposite side, the hall gave way to the hollow center of the tower, which was a sight beyond all comprehension. The tower was a vast cylinder, projecting forever upward, and I dare say that the hollow interior was at least two miles across and could have held a small city within it. The inner wall of the cylinder was riddled with innumerable balconies and doorways, where more of the creatures could be seen moving about. Each doorway glowed with its own unique color of light, which when gazed upon from a distance created a beguiling pattern of luminous colors that gradually faded into the distance along the inward curving wall of the enormous cylinder.

The most staggering vision yet came to me when I turned my gaze upward. So tall was the tower that the wall, twinkling with the colored lights of its doorways, gradually receded into the distance and finally appeared as nothing more than grey mist, as if looking into distant fog. The most striking sight to behold, however, was the vast number of objects flying about in this space. I ascertained that the objects were vessels of some sort, as I saw the three-legged creatures entering and exiting them on the ground floor and on the balconies. The flying vessels were perfectly spherical, and like the doorways, they each glowed with their own particular color. However, it was the extraordinary number of them, and the rapid and haphazard manner in which they flew that I found to be so bewildering. As I gazed upward into the atmosphere of the tower, the flying vessels resembled a swarm of thousands of fireflies of every possible color, flying about such that they must surely collide, causing great harm to the passengers within them. However, no such collisions seemed to occur.

By this time I had become convinced that these visions were much more than a mere dream, as even at my most imaginative and intellectual moments I could never have conceived of such magnificent and mystifying products of industrial achievement. These visions were being shown to me, as if some grand being with power equal to that of God Himself wished for me to witness them. Further evidence that these visions were arranged and intentional was provided by the fact that each time I was presented with a sight requiring some time to observe and ponder the significance, my flying motion stopped as if to allow this. Thus, having paused just so long as needed for my appraisal of the tower's grand interior, I began flying upward.

I cannot say what distance may have passed as I rose swiftly up the tower, other than that it was many miles. And still the endless balconies bustled with the activities of thousands of inhabitants. It confounded my mind to attempt to comprehend the size of the structure and the population it held within it, particularly considering that I had seen additional such towers in the distance before entering this one.

Finally, after what seemed to be many minutes of rising upward, I abruptly changed direction and entered another horizontal corridor, which had the same appearance and bustling of occupants as the first one. This corridor, however, led me back out to the tower's exterior. Upon exiting the tower, I saw that I was higher above the ground than any man had ever been. The ground was so far below that I could discern no features other than the largest bodies of water and mountains. And above, rather than the pink sky that I had previously observed, was a black sky filled with stars. And still the tower extended far above me as I continued rising upward beside its exterior surface. Finally I saw the tower's lofty summit. Its top was joined to the vast web of horizontal threads I had seen from far below. From my position I could see three of these threads attached to the distal end of the tower. The angles of these three threads suggested to me that there were three more I could not see extending from the other side.

As I neared the top of the tower, it became apparent that each of the horizontal threads of the web was as large in diameter as the tower itself. Again I wondered how such mass could be held so high above the world without falling and crashing to the ground.

At last I flew above the tower's summit and changed direction again. Flying toward the center of the enormous circular roof, I saw something remarkable happening there. A cloud of tiny particles slowly rose from the tower's roof and disappeared into the starry heavens. As I drew nearer, however, the particles were larger than I had thought. They were in fact each of them several feet in diameter, and they were flying from hundreds of openings in the tower's arched roof. I finally came to rest beside one of these openings. A platform slowly appeared out of the hole, and upon it was something I recognized. It was a lump of clay, exactly like that which I had encountered in the village of my captors.

Suddenly, by some hidden mechanical operation below, the platform was thrust upward by a pole to which it was attached, thus tossing the object with considerable force toward the stars above.

The last I remember of this most extraordinary vision was watching as the lump of clay continued flying into the heavens among thousands of others that were being released in a similar way.

That was the vision that appeared to me in the night. I may refer to it as a dream, for want of a better word, but I do not believe I was truly sleeping during the process. I have written this in an attempt to better understand it. Perhaps you will draw a different conclusion than I have. However, at this time, after contemplating all that I have recently witnessed and experienced, and assuming that the wondrous visions were not merely dreams of my mind's creation, I can think of no better explanation than the following. The lump of clay present in this village is not a natural phenomenon of this world. Instead, it originated on another world, upon which exists a civilization far greater than that of modern men. Like the other industrial achievements of this greater civilization, the lump of clay possesses properties that bewilder the intellect of a man such as myself, as I am certain it would of any other man of this world.

You may conclude that a place of vast towers rising into the heavens must surely be the Kingdom of God. I must disagree. This is not to say that I believe God does not exist, however I must acknowledge that the grand achievements often attributed to God's hand are stories created by the minds of men. These stories, although they inspire and stir the intentions of innumerable civilized people, are of acts, beings, and objects that are incorporeal and nonmaterial. On the other hand, the achievements of industry I have seen in my visions are physical structures built by corporeal beings. I now believe that somewhere in the heavens is a world where these astonishing structures exist, and I intend to learn whatever I can of the mysterious lump of clay that originated there.

THE SECOND EVENT that changed the way I view the world occurred in the morning, following the aforementioned vision. Upon awaking I was quite pleased to discover that my health had continued to improve. I still felt no pain in the areas of my injuries, and I had retained the capability to recall every past moment of my life. It is scarcely possible to overstate the pleasing benefits of this last condition, as I believe I could be quite content to sit alone for days as I recall in great detail all that I have ever learned and previously forgotten. I do not know for certain to what specific ingredient I owe for this astounding capability, but I now suspect all of my health benefits are a result of laying my hands upon the object that now occupies my thoughts and dreams, the mysterious lump of clay. If I could take this object into my possession and somehow transport it out of this primeval forest and back to London, I can only imagine how it might change that civilized society. If it could benefit others as it has me, then the medical profession would be greatly transformed. Likewise would the profession of education be transformed, as students would retain all that they read and all that they hear spoken.

As if the natives could sense my thoughts lingering on the lump of clay, Sinanie, Matiinuo, and two others came to my hut in the morning and took me again to confront it. I was forced at spear point to descend the ladder and walk to the same clearing where I had been savagely maimed three days before. The lump of clay was then carried out in the same manner as before and placed on the ground before me.

I looked around at the dozen or so Papuan natives gathered there. At first I thought all of them were men, but then I saw one woman. She was standing partially hidden behind one of the men, gazing timidly at me over his shoulder. She was the first female of the tribe I had seen. Her breasts were exposed for all to see, but she wore a cord about her waist from which hung a tightly bunched mat of grass fibers that somewhat covered her reproductive area. Her long, frizzly hair was neatly drawn back and tied into a clump at the back of her head. Numerous cords were tied to the clump of hair and were looped around to the front. Fastened to these cords were a variety of amulets and talismans carved from bone and wood, each of them hanging at a different position between her breasts. This was a pleasing arrangement of ornaments, and like the men around her, she bore the youthful skin of a child upon the body of an adult of indeterminate age.

Matiinuo pointed to the lump of clay, and he said, "*Lamotelokhai.*"

"Lam-oh-tell-oh-kai," I repeated slowly. It appeared the tribe had a name for the lump of clay. It seemed to me to have the sound of something of grand importance, suitable to what I already knew of the object.

The men pressed several spear points to my skin to guide me toward it but did not draw blood, which suggested that, at least for the moment, they were no longer interested in causing me injury or pain. I complied, as it was my wish to learn more about the object anyway. I kneeled and put my hands upon the lump of clay, the Lamotelokhai. A cluster of hundreds of the strange figures appeared as an illusion before my eyes, suspended there as if hanging by threads too thin to be seen. One of the figures moved to the side, followed by three more that moved into position just above it. But I was no longer interested in completing mathematical patterns, as I was prepared to test an hypothesis I had developed following my previous encounter with the Lamotelokhai.

Three days before, when I had been pushed to the limits of my endurance, I had cried out to the object for mercy, thinking that God's presence was within it. And then a miracle had occurred, or so it had seemed. I now determined, based upon that experience, to simply speak to the object.

"From whence have you come?" said I.

Suddenly I no longer was kneeling on the ground in a remote village. Instead, I was back in my previous vision, suspended in the air above a red-hued landscape of rocks and pools of swirling water. In the distance was the tall, thin outline of one of the towers, extending upward and disappearing into the haze of the sky. This was the same place I had visited in my dream, however this time the vision was much more immersive and hypnotic. All of my senses were engaged with stimuli, such as sounds of the water beneath me rippling from the movements of swimming creatures, the warm wind against my skin, and a most overpowering aroma of some unknown and caustic substance in the air itself as it entered my nose and mouth. I was only barely aware that I had ever existed outside of the vision. To make matters worse, confusing images flowed into my mind. I could not understand most of them, however they seemed to be related to the world that I was observing, such as different continents upon it, and how the three-legged inhabitants used the resources of the world to create their towers. Then, suddenly, the vision ended. I was again upon my knees, at the mercy of a dozen savage natives.

So great was the shock of this abrupt assault upon my senses that I nearly toppled over. I recovered my balance and sat motionless for some time, attempting to align my thoughts into some coherent path. Finally, I was able to consider the implications of what had happened. I had spoken a request, and somehow the object had understood and responded by placing a most vivid vision in my mind. But this vision had been so much more than the dreams I had experienced, perhaps because my hands had been resting directly upon the clay. I looked down at my hands. They were now shaking, and I pressed them firmly to the pliant clay to steady them. I attempted to think clearly. It occurred to me that perhaps I should avoid asking further questions, lest I again become overwhelmed. But I was caught in the grip of profound curiosity.

"From whence have I come?" I asked.

Again, a vision flooded my mind. I found myself standing on Hertford Street in Mayfair, London, gazing at the terrace house of my parents, where I had been born and had lived as a child. A carriage passed by me, and I heard the muffled conversation of two gentlemen within it. I smelled the sweat of the horses. It was as if I were there, in the same spot I had stood so many times as a boy. The vision ended, and again I was left reeling from the shock of it. After taking a moment to becalm my mental faculties, it occurred to me that this time I had recovered more quickly, perhaps because the vision had been of a place with which I was already familiar. Or perhaps more experience with such visions made them easier to endure. Following this conjecture, which I now know to be false, I formulated yet another question.

"How is it possible that my grievous wounds came to be healed in only three days?"

Suddenly, it was as if my consciousness had broken free of my physical self and floated away. I was looking at my own body, as if I had become a tiny mosquito and was flying about. With a force apparently beyond my control, I flew to the place where my hand rested upon the Lamotelokhai's surface. As I moved closer, it seemed as if I were the tiniest of specks, and my own hand loomed before me as large as a mountain. I approached even closer, until the skin of my hand stretched out before me like a vast landscape of hills and valleys and hairs, which were standing like tall trees. I then passed directly into the skin, and I was surrounded by things completely foreign and strange to me. Cells of the tissues of my hand were enormous, and I passed through them freely. I beheld myriads of particles and filaments of all shapes and of unknown purpose. I finally reached a place which I was certain was the point of contact between my palm and the lump of clay. I was sure of this because, although the clay consisted of particles of varying shapes, all of them were of distinct symmetrical form, as if they had been produced in a factory rather than by a process of nature. Flowing into my living tissue from the symmetrical components of the clay was a river of small particles, all of them of the same size and appearance. Each of them had the shape of a cube, but with cylinder-like appendages protruding outward from each of the cube's eight corners. Thousands of these particles steadily flowed from the uniform components of the clay into the irregular components of my hand's interior. I fell in behind them, following them as they made their way through endless vast and peculiar landscapes of the inner workings of my own body.

At last the symmetrical objects arrived at a place that was apparently their final destination, upon which they began a most astounding process. Before me was an area of obviously violent destruction. Instead of the organized and intricate structure of the healthy tissues I had passed through to get here, this area was a scene of complete disarray. Cells were torn open, their contents spilling out and being swept away by rivers of fluid. Particles of filth and dirt, of all sizes and shapes, were everywhere, tumbling about or firmly embedded in ruined tissue. Upon arriving by the thousands at this scene of destruction, the machine-like objects wasted no time. Moving at a rate my mind could scarcely comprehend, they attached themselves to the ruined tissue. Wherever one would attach, others would immediately attach to it in a very orderly fashion, like interlocking pieces of a puzzle, stacking upon each other, layer upon layer. And then, as I watched in astonishment, each of the stacked objects seemed to shift its own shape and change its own composition, until together they resembled the very tissues to which they had attached themselves. This process continued, until at last the entire area was organized and intricate. It was healthy tissue once again.

The grand vision ended as abruptly as it had begun. I looked about in confusion, having completely forgotten where I was. The Papuan natives still stood around me in a circle, watching me. I tried to say something, but I could form no words. I sensed that my hands were trembling, and I looked down at them. Without knowing it, at some point I had clenched them into fists and in the process had pulled handfuls of clay loose from the large lump. Raw scratches could be seen on my palms where my unkempt fingernails had torn the skin. I opened my fists and gazed at the clay I had pulled loose. Before my eyes it disappeared as it was absorbed through my skin into my body.

As if they understood that my mind had been overcome with more splendorous sights than most men had ever seen in a lifetime, the natives lifted me to my feet and guided me back to my hut.

For much of the afternoon I lay naked upon the floor, trying without appreciable success to force my mind to function as it should. At last I recovered enough to sit up and attempt to write the details of my experiences.

I am now more determined than ever to learn what I can of this Lamotelokhai, but I must be more cautious. It is quite possible that learning of its extraordinary properties too quickly could drive a man to utter madness.

12

APRIL 28, 1868

MUCH HAS HAPPENED in the four days since I last wrote. In order to simplify the telling, I will first describe my progress with the Lamotelokhai, followed by some pertinent observations of the nature of the tribe to which I now seem to be inextricably bound.

I continue to get the sense that these natives regard my work with the Lamotelokhai as something of importance to them. They have taken me to it every day, as if this were integral to some schedule only they are privy to. It should not be long before I can ask them to explain this, as I am quickly learning the basics of their language, a task greatly facilitated by my new and extraordinary gift of recollection.

I was again taken to the Lamotelokhai on the day following my last notebook entry. The natives carried their spears, however they did not use them for coercion, as I knew precisely what to do and was quite willing. I had carefully formulated some questions for the object in such a way that I would not again be overcome by an onslaught of bewildering visions. Or so I had hoped.

Again on my knees, naked, and surrounded by Papuan observers, I wasted no time. I placed my hands upon the lump of clay, resulting in a vision of several hundred of the strange figures. I ignored them and asked my first question.

"Are you what the natives here call Lamotelokhai?"

Before I could prepare myself for what I knew would come next, I had already been transported to a rocky shore beside the sea. Immediately my senses were nearly overpowered by the stiff ocean breeze, the sounds of waves striking the shore, and the smell of salt water and rotting aquatic plants among the rocks. Several Papuan men stood before me, but they did not seem to see me, and I watched them as if I were an invisible phantom. One of them I recognized to be Mati-inuo, although he was without his white feathers. Other than that, he appeared much as he does today, with youthful skin and clear eyes. However, the men with him were in a far worse state, showing the usual ravages of uncivilized life. They appeared to suffer from starvation and perhaps other privations, their ribs and knee bones clearly outlined by withered and contorted skin. Thick effluence seeped from their blood-shotten eyes, which were sunken within their sockets. Matiinuo and his companions gazed down at something on the ground. It was the Lamotelokhai, somewhat misshapen in order to conform to the rocks and sand upon which it rested. Matiinuo reached for it, pulled loose a handful, and gave a portion of it to each of his companions. After some little hesitation they ate their portions. They continued gazing at the clay for a time, and then Matiinuo spoke to the men.

"*Khakhul-fekho lép-telo. Alümon-fekho khil-telo. Nu be khomilo-n-din-da. If-é lelua laléo ganggail khendil. If-é laléo umo nu é-fu. If-é laléo mekho nu damo. If-é laléo mekho gekhené damo. Nokhu-lekhé laimekho if-é lop, laléo-tekhé damo-nu lefül abül yu la-khe-bené fa-lu-lo khendil. Ati-lo, Lamotelokhai. Nu laléo-fi alip Lamotelokhai."*

My translation (added when transcribing this notebook):
"Today you are ill. Tomorrow you will be healthy. It is impossible that you die. This clay is a spirit with much magic power. This spirit talks to me when I sleep. This spirit put knowledge (information) into me. This spirit will also put knowledge into you. We must take this clay into the forest and hide it, because the spirit has told me that in time someone will come and take away this magic. When they take away this magic, the world will end. I will name this spirit Lamotelokhai."

The vision ended, and I was back in the village, blinking my eyes and trying to hold my balance, as even the briefest of such visions was staggering to behold. I had not understood all of Matiinuo's words in the vision, but it did seem clear that I was being shown that he had indeed given the object the name, Lamotelokhai.

However, I had not anticipated that a seemingly simple question would result in such an overpowering vision. Upon contemplating my next question, I decided that even more caution would be wise.

"What is my name?"

Before I had even spoken the complete sentence, I was transported back to my hut, at the precise time when I had introduced myself to Matiinuo and Sinanie. Again I was gazing at the two men, afraid and uncertain of their intentions. And again I put my hand to my chest and spoke my name. "Samuel."

This time, when the vision ended, I recovered more quickly, perhaps because this vision had been brief. Perhaps also because it was a scene that was familiar to me, or because it was a question for which I already knew the answer.

I considered for a moment that these two visions had begun before I had even completed my questions. I had no ideas for how this could be possible, but I realized that perhaps I did not need to speak my questions aloud at all. Thus I formulated my next question only in my mind, mentally saying the words as I often do when I read to myself.

"Are you a living organism, or are you some manner of machine?"

I steadied myself to endure the vision, in case this new method had the same effect. Then it was upon me. I suddenly found myself hovering in the air in a vast chamber, with white luminous walls far in the distance. All manner of apparatuses and machines filled the chamber. Some of them were small, while others were as large as a house. Some of them were built with obvious solid, mechanical parts, while others seemed to be filled with various liquids. The entire chamber bustled with the industrious activity of hundreds of the strange three-legged creatures I had seen in my dream. The creatures moved about with apparent purpose around the apparatuses. It seemed to me to be a factory of some kind, although there was not a single item of machinery for which I had any idea of its purpose.

I then flew through the open air of the chamber until I was near one of the walls, which bulged outward as if the chamber were a huge flattened bubble. Near the wall was a white structure that was larger than most of the other machines. It was irregularly shaped and rounded, such that there were no corners or straight edges, and its tallest rounded bulge was perhaps thirty feet high. At one end of the structure, dozens of the creatures were gathered as if waiting for something to happen.

As I drew nearer, I saw that something was indeed happening. There was a round opening in the structure, and the white walls around the opening moved of their own accord as if made of pliable India rubber. The entire flexible perimeter of the opening contracted, causing the hole in the center to be pushed away from the main body of the structure. Oddly, this looked to me like the anus of a gigantic white earthworm, with muscles contracting in an attempt to push out a particle of waste. And just as this somewhat revolting thought occurred to me, an object did indeed appear from the opening. There was no mistaking the object. It was a large lump of clay, the Lamotelokhai, or one of the thousands like it I had seen in my dream. Before the object fell to the floor, the nearest of the three-legged creatures held out a thin tray beneath it. At that moment I realized for the first time that, in addition to having two legs in the rear and one very slender leg near the head, these creatures also had two small, frail-looking arms, attached to the body on either side of the anterior slender leg. Holding the tray out with one of its diminutive hands, the creature accepted the clay, and somehow the tray supported it, notwithstanding the fact that the large lump appeared to be far too heavy. The creature then carried the clay, balanced upon the small tray, away to some unknown destination. I watched as another lump was pushed from the opening and carried off in a similar way by another of the creatures, and then another after that.

The vision ended, and I caught myself before falling over onto the ground at the feet of the observing natives. This last vision had been more than I had bargained for, and I feared that this day's session with the Lamotelokhai might come to an early end, as there seemed to be a limit as to how many of these mesmerizing visions my mind could endure before becoming utterly dazed and useless. I contemplated what I had seen as I becalmed myself. I was still confused regarding my question. I had witnessed these objects being produced in a place I had believed to be a factory, but the actual process of their final stage of creation had seemed oddly natural and animal-like. Nevertheless, it was clear that the three-legged creatures had supervised their production and were ultimately responsible for what became of them afterwards.

Before long I had recovered my balance and wits sufficiently as to increase my confidence, which then caused me to set aside my previous determination to be cautious. In my excitement, I desired to learn more of these strange creatures that seemed capable of hitherto unimagined feats. I hastily expressed a new request in my mind without speaking it aloud.

"In my visions I have seen a strange world. Upon this world were creatures, moving about within towers that reached beyond the sky. And I saw these creatures laboring in a factory, producing objects such as that which I now touch with my hands. I would like to learn more about these creatures."

This proved to be a grave mistake, as I had forgotten to ask only questions of a very specific nature, which would have limited the scope of the Lamotelokhai's response. However, it was too late. My mind was flooded with visions so grand and numerous that I could not possibly comprehend it all. There were visions of every intricate detail of the external and internal anatomy of the three-legged creatures. Their bodies were so foreign to my understanding that I had no choice but to allow the scenes to flash by me without the slightest comprehension. I had somewhat more success with visions regarding social matters. There were examples of relations between individuals and groups, some of them more complex than I had thought possible. There were scenes of rituals, official proceedings, administering of justice, educating the young and old alike, social gatherings, means of determining consensus among large populations in order to make important decisions, and activities in which they engaged for amusement. There were visions of artistic achievements and endeavors of enterprise and industry. And there was much more, but I could only endure the smallest fragment of it before my mind began to fail, and then I was aware of only occasional pieces of these lessons. I became terrified that the flood of visions would never stop, and I fell into the grip of panic. Just when I was at the thin edge of my sanity, the visions came to an end. I was only scarcely aware that I had fallen to the ground, and I could provide no assistance to the natives as they dragged me to my hut and hoisted my weakened and useless body up to it.

For what seemed like many hours I lay upon the floor staring at the rafters, unable to sleep and yet unable to shape my thoughts to any useful purpose. This condition persisted the rest of the day and through the night. On several occasions I soiled myself. I was unable to prevent it and likewise was unable to command my body to even roll away from it.

Sinanie and two other men entered my hut some time after the sun had come up. They kindly cleaned my body and the floor, and they dragged me a few feet to the side. They forced me to drink water from a gourd. This seemed to help, because after they went away I slept tranquilly.

When I awoke it was late in the afternoon, and I realized that I felt much better. I got to my feet and paced about the hut, as my body had become bruised from lying motionless upon the bamboo floor. It occurred to me that the only thing that had prevented my passing into complete madness, or perhaps even dying, was that I had fallen upon the ground, thus releasing my hold upon the Lamotelokhai and terminating the visions. However, I had learned many things from those visions, notwithstanding the fact that I had absorbed only a small fraction of what had been shown to me. I now had a great deal of knowledge of the three-legged creatures, the creators of the Lamotelokhai. I found the particulars of the structure and function of their bodies to be altogether bewildering, as I could make little sense of what I had seen. However, it was the nature of their society that most interested me.

I have lived my life in the greatest civilized society in the world. However, the most educated men, with whom I dare to include myself, would argue that we have not yet come close to what we imagine to be the epitome of social progress. This "perfect social state" that we imagine involves equality of all members of society, with respect to wealth and opportunities to pursue that which brings pleasure and comfort to each individual. Such equality is so easily imagined, and yet it is so difficult to achieve. This, I am sure, is due to aspects of our "civilized" society that many have struggled so hard to establish and therefore would struggle equally to preserve. Perhaps the most obvious aspect is the accumulation of wealth. It is the dream of many men to accumulate wealth in order to rise above the general population, to be considered wealthy, and to claim the property and privileges that accompany that title. However, the reality is that this leads to great inequality, as only a few can achieve such wealth, while the vast majority must suffer in ways too numerous to count.

During the agonizing minutes in which I had witnessed visions of the three-legged creatures' society, one thing was made clear to me, that those creatures had achieved a level of equality of which modern men can only dream. Each individual creature was free to pursue activities, occupations, and professions that most interested him, often changing professions at will as his interests progressed over time. Every achievement, including construction of the vast towers and the tunnels in the sky, was for the good of the entire population, and was accomplished because there were sufficient numbers of individuals interested in making it so. Every individual enjoyed the same rights and privileges and had access to what he needed in order to live in good health and happiness. There seemed to be no expectation of, nor any great yearning for, accumulation of wealth beyond that of any other individual.

It is my belief that the progression of any group of people begins with a state of pure savagery, which then, given suitable time and resources, gradually progresses to agriculture and industry, with the inevitable result of accumulated wealth for the few and suffering of the many. But my belief extends beyond this arguably inadequate state of society, as such a civilization will surely crumble if it does not eventually progress to a state of equality for all individuals such as I have witnessed in my visions.

Having myself come from a family of some wealth, this may seem to be an argument rife with hypocrisy and contrary to my station in life. However, I am only one of many educated and cultured men who believe this to be the highest state of civilization, and I would be quite willing to redistribute my share of my family's resources if only the great civilization of England were upon the verge of such enlightened transformation. Sadly, though, I fear that the realization of such change will not occur during my brief lifetime, as there are far too many wealthy men in England who do not share this vision.

Although I shall not live to see such a future as this, I am much encouraged to have witnessed evidence that it is quite possible to achieve.

FOR THE REMAINDER of that day I slowly recovered my strength by pacing about while further contemplating the bewildering visions that had nearly killed me. Sinanie came to my hut with another man, whom he introduced as Ahea. Like the other men I had seen, Ahea wore a gourd upon his sexual organ. Other than that and a few braided cords around his neck, the only adornment he wore was a headdress made of the fur of a mammal, perhaps a cuscus. At first I feared these men had come to take me to another of my sessions with the Lamotelokhai, for which I certainly was not ready—at least not yet. Instead they placed sago paste and water on the floor before me and then watched in silence as I consumed them.

It wasn't until yesterday, April 27, that I was again taken to the Lamotelokhai. The natives did not seem to care that my previous encounter with it had been so costly to my mental wellbeing. As before, after bringing out the Lamotelokhai and setting it beside me, they stood around me and waited for whatever might happen next. However, I had determined to avoid further harm, and upon placing my hands on the lump of clay I silently expressed my first request.

"Lamotelokhai, I would like to learn from you in ways that do not involve placing visions into my mind. I beg you to show me no more visions, for I am too feeble to endure them!"

I waited, not knowing if such a request would be granted or even understood. The only thing that happened was that the strange figures floating before my eyes disappeared. I concluded that this was the Lamotelokhai responding to my desperate request, and so I proceeded as I had planned.

"I have seen that you healed my injuries, and I have seen that you set on fire wooden spears embedded within my body. I wish to make requests so that I might learn what other deeds you are capable of."

I then pulled a small portion of the clay free. I looked around at the natives and saw that the man standing next to Sinanie held a spear. I pointed at the spear and held out my hand for him to pass it to me. The man hesitated and then exchanged a few words with Sinanie, after which he extended the point so that I could grasp it, which I did, smearing the clay upon the tip.

I then formed in my mind a request. "Can you put fire to this spear?"

Before I even had the chance to release the spear, it ignited. I quickly withdrew my scorched hand and rubbed the palm into the dirt beneath me to soothe it. The man gazed in wonder at his burning spear for a moment and then put out the fire on the ground. This resulted in excited talking among the natives. I found this to be puzzling, as it now seemed to me that requesting such a thing from the Lamotelokhai was a simple matter, and surely they had learned before this day to make such requests.

I was much encouraged by this success. Although I had deemed it necessary, I had understood that asking the lump of clay to never again show me visions would limit what I could learn from it. However, now it seemed there was still much I could learn without the risk of conjuring visions that could cost me my sanity.

Next I placed a bit of the clay upon a birthmark I had always had on the back of my right hand.

"You have shown me that you can send machine-like objects into my body to repair my injuries. Can you repair this imperfection of my skin?"

I felt prickling on my hand before I had finished forming this silent request. I waited patiently. Some minutes later, the birthmark began changing its size and color, and before long it was not visible at all. In its place was healthy and pale skin, with normal hairs protruding from it rather than the abnormal long and black hairs that had grown there before.

The natives were much less impressed with this than they had been with the burning spear. I, however, perhaps due to my more advanced knowledge of civilized medical science and the intricate nature of healing, was duly impressed regarding such an operation.

Again I was encouraged by my success and was beginning to realize the immense possibilities. Hence, I made a slightly larger request. First I spread the clay onto my beard, which had grown quite wildly, as I had not shaved since I had last been in my house on Humboldt Bay. Having noted that my previous requests had been granted before I had even finished forming the words in my mind, I decided to try making a request without expressing silent words at all. Instead, I simply formed a mental depiction of my clean-shaven face.

Although I could not see my own face, it felt as if tiny ants were crawling about on it, reminding me of the night my wounds had healed as I tried to sleep. For a few minutes I resisted touching my face, but soon I was overcome with fears that something might go terribly wrong, resulting in my disfigurement, and I could not stop myself from putting both hands to my face. If the process had involved any pain, I am sure I would have cried out in panic, but I becalmed myself, and soon it was over. My face was then perfectly smooth, as if I had just had it shaved in the finest London barber's shop. This time the natives were indeed impressed, resulting in much talking and pointing.

As I prepared to make my next request, a most peculiar thing happened. A tree kangaroo walked between the legs of the natives and stopped at my side. I was quite sure it was the same creature Charles had shot on the ill-fated day of his murder. The tree kangaroo gazed at me for a moment with the same countenance I had seen before, one of mild curiosity, although I assume this description to be of my mind's invention. It then faced the nearest natives, sat up on its haunches, and began moving its forepaws about in the same intricate manner as before. Even more than before, I was convinced that this was a silent language of some kind, as the gesticulations seemed too precise to be otherwise. The natives watched this strange behavior with no particular expression on their faces, as if this were something they saw every day. After about a minute of this, the creature dropped back down upon all four feet and walked through the natives' legs again. They allowed it to go without harming it.

This unusual exchange apparently brought an end to my session with the Lamotelokhai. Sinanie waved for me to stand up. Then, to my surprise, several of the men led me to a hut that was not my own. Two women were in the hut. They were similar in appearance to the woman I had seen several days before. They were surprised at my sudden presence and looked as if they might run away at any moment. However, Sinanie spoke to them, and with whispered remarks to each other and disdainful glances at me, they returned to their tasks. They were creating sago. Sinanie spoke to me as he pointed out various items and procedures, as if I were a student there for the purpose of learning of their indigenous culture.

The sago tree is a palm, of great thickness but not as high as a typical cocoa-nut tree. The sago has immense spiny leaves, sometimes fifteen feet long, which are used for many purposes. However, it is the pithy center of the broad trunk that is processed into sago, a staple food used by some hundreds of thousands of people of the Malay Archipelago. Assuming Sinanie's tribe prepared sago in a way similar to Penapul's Humboldt Bay tribe, the pith of the tree's trunk would have first been cut from the tree where the tree had fallen, and then this pith would have been washed in a stream and kneaded until all that remained was a dense paste, or raw sago. It was this raw sago that these women worked with as I watched. A fire burned in one corner, and above it, suspended upon shelves made of clay, lumps of raw sago dried in the fire's heat. Woven baskets that contained hard lumps of sago that had previously been dried sat next to the two women. The women were using rounded rocks to pound these hard lumps into fine powder. I assumed that this fine, dry powder could be stored for long periods of time and then mixed with water as needed, thus producing the rather tasteless sago paste that they had fed to me. It puzzled me why these natives did not bake this paste into sago cakes, which I knew to be a common way to prepare it and a way that was to my liking. However, with my limited use of their language I could not effectively ask them this.

As we descended the ladder from the hut, the man Ahea waited for us on the ground. He offered me some cooked meat and a plantain. Until this time I had consumed only sago paste, which certainly would sustain me but was quite bland. Thus I readily accepted these and consumed them at that very moment as if I were a starving beast. The natives laughed and pointed at me, apparently amused by this.

I was then taken to yet another hut, where a man I had not seen before sat upon the floor, carefully carving a small piece of wood with a sharpened bone. Numerous talismans, amulets, and other objects he had evidently already carved were neatly arranged on the floor. And there were stones, pieces of wood, and dried gourds, perhaps waiting to be carved.

As Sinanie pointed and talked, for this was apparently another lesson, I kneeled and inspected the completed objects more closely. I was struck by the artistry of each of them. The man, whose name I was told was Noadi, was highly skilled. There were small carvings of various animals, including several that appeared to be tree kangaroos, although they were of a peculiar artistic style, such as I had seen with carvings on totem poles in the museums of London. Next to these lay two spears with sharpened and fire-hardened points. Most striking, however, was that upon their shafts were carved the very same figures I had seen floating in the air before my eyes when I had put my hands upon the Lamotelokhai. I then saw that these same figures were carved into the surfaces of several hollow gourds scattered among the objects on the floor. These gourds were of the type the men wore upon their sexual organs. I picked up one of the gourds and held it out to

Sinanie, also pointing to the figures carved upon his own gourd.

"I have seen these figures, when I touch the Lamotelokhai," said I.

He replied, *"Kho-Lamotelokhai di gekhené alip maf. Masekha doleli di nokhu alip maf. Gekhené, laléo, di alip maf Lamotelokhai."*

———

My translation (added when transcribing this notebook):

"The Lamotelokhai talks to you with those shapes (pictures). It is to invoke taboo for us to talk with those shapes. But you, outsider, talk to the Lamotelokhai with those shapes."

———

Although I had scarcely tried speaking them myself, by this time I had learned some of the words of this tribe's curious language. The word *'di'* was a reference to 'talking,' the word *'gekhené'* was a way of saying 'you,' and the word *'maf'* meant something regarding a picture. Sinanie, I believe, was referring to the Lamotelokhai talking to me with pictures. Beyond that I could make little sense of what he had said.

Noadi picked up one of the slender gourds that had not yet been carved with figures. He spoke a few words and pointed to my sexual organ, which was still exposed for all to see. I had become so accustomed to my naked state and loss of dignity that I did not at first realize he meant for me to wear the gourd. I accepted the gift. The men in the hut quietly watched, apparently waiting for me to put it on, but I had not the slightest idea of how this was done, nor how the contrivance would stay in place once I began walking about. One reason for my confusion was that, unlike the men of the Humboldt Bay tribe, who used cords around their waists to secure their gourds upon their privates, Sinanie and his fellow tribesmen had no cords in place for such purpose. Hence, their gourds were prone to swinging from side to side as they walked.

I looked from the gourd in my hand to those worn by the natives before me, at which point they began a hearty roar of laughter. I was in no mood for such humiliation, and I held out the gourd to return it to Noadi. Instead of accepting it, he stood up and pulled his own gourd away from his body until it came off with a rather revolting sound. It was then that I realized how these men kept their gourds from slipping off. They not only inserted their sexual organ into the gourd, but also they stuffed the scrotum and its two occupants inside, thus making all of this so tight that the gourd could only be removed with some force. Noadi stuffed the contents back into his gourd, making the process look quite easy. I tried it myself, resulting in even more hearty laughter, which in turn made me so determined to succeed that I finally accomplished the task. This involved no small measure of pain, but I refused to display any evidence of this that might produce further mockery.

I managed to muster an attitude of defiance. "I see that you find this to be amusing," I said to Sinanie. "At least you could tell me what you call these ridiculous adornments." I then pointed to my gourd and said, "*Fi*," which was their word for 'name.'

Sinanie pointed to his own gourd and replied, "*Mbayap*." He then pointed to mine and said, "*Mbayap-lena*." I knew the word '*lena*' to mean 'small.'

This began another round of exuberant merriment.

THOSE WERE the notable events of yesterday, April 27. Today I was taken from my hut for yet another session with the Lamotelokhai, which was followed by another lesson on the culture and language of these indigenes. It now seems scarcely possible that only a few days ago they seemed intent on maiming and killing me. I do not know for certain the reason that their treatment of me has changed as it has, but it seems likely to be a result of my progress with the Lamotelokhai. The natives wish for me to learn what I can of it, although to what consequence I can only guess. This is fortunate for me, as I now have no other desire so great as to understand more of what it can do.

It is certainly true, I must add, that I wish to survive this ordeal and someday return to London to see my parents, my friends, and my betrothed, Lindsey. I yearn for their company, and I have no desire to expire here in the wilderness without returning to them, and without informing others of what is hidden here. Perhaps I may eventually be capable of formulating a request for the Lamotelokhai to help me escape this village and take it with me to civilization. However, until that is possible, my place is here, among the savages who nearly killed me.

When I was taken today from my hut, instead of leading me to the clearing where I had previously worked with the Lamotelokhai, the natives led me to yet another hut I had not yet seen. When we climbed the ladder to the hut, I saw there the lump of clay, resting upon its carrying platform, which in turn rested upon a short bamboo table. The table, only about knee high, stood in the middle of the room, and living vines were growing up its legs and over every inch of its surface. Tendrils and stems of the vines intertwined with the bamboo in such a way that, until looking more closely, I thought perhaps the table itself was a living plant.

Sinanie gestured for me to approach the table, indicating that today I was to have my lesson in this hut. I had not anticipated such an arrangement, thus I used some gesticulations and words I had learned to explain that I wished to leave the hut before beginning. He seemed to understand, and he followed closely as I went to the ground and collected several small stones. I then looked about under some fallen branches and rotten trunks until I located a large stag beetle, which I carefully captured and handed over to Sinanie, indicating to him that I wanted it kept alive. Finally, I picked up a few sticks and pulled a small plant from the soil, and we returned to the hut where the Lamotelokhai and three other natives awaited.

For my first experiment I placed a stone upon the table beside the lump of clay. I rested my hands on the clay and formed a vision in my mind, in which I imagined the stone breaking apart into fine sand. I pulled off some of the clay and smeared it onto the stone. After perhaps a minute of waiting, the stone cracked into two pieces with a sharp pop. Each of the halves then cracked into two more, and each of those into two. Before long the pieces cracking apart were too small to see, although I still heard innumerable faint pops as they broke apart. In place of the stone there was now a pile of sand.

My next request was a bold one, which I was doubtful could be achieved. I placed a second stone on the table, put my hands on the clay, and formed a vision of the stone transforming into gold. I smeared a pinch of clay upon the stone and waited. Soon the stone's color began changing, until finally it was the very color of gold. I picked it up, only to discover that it was no heavier than before. It was most certainly not gold. Either my request was not understood, or the task was simply beyond the capabilities of the Lamotelokhai. Thus I put words to my request.

"I wish for the entire nature of this stone to become gold. Gold is a metal, which is much heavier than the minerals that make up this stone. Gold, in fact, is the heaviest of all metals. Can you do this?"

I then anointed the stone with more clay and waited. The stone's shape began to change, imperceptibly at first and then more quickly, until it resembled melted gold, its surface shiny and smooth. I held my hand above it and felt no heat. When I picked it up, the lower side was imprinted with the contours of the tabletop, as if it had indeed melted there and then cooled and hardened. It was now less than half the size of the original stone, and based upon its weight, I could only conclude that it was gold. Needless to say, I was quite delighted over this. However, at the same time, I experienced an ominous sense of dread. I had made this request as a result of my scientific curiosity, but others would view it with quite different motives. This ability was the kind of thing that men were inclined to fight wars over.

Alas, I hadn't time to ponder on such matters, as I did not wish to squander the short time I was allowed with the Lamotelokhai. I had determined to discover what I could regarding the effects of the clay upon living things other than myself. I beckoned Sinanie to bring me the stag beetle, which he had kept alive in his hands. I took the beetle and placed it upon the table. It was an impressive insect, rusty in color and nearly four inches long. Half this length was comprised of two massive mandibles, looking somewhat like the antlers of a deer. The beetle began walking about the tabletop.

This time I tried making a request by combining expressed words with a mental vision. "I wish to change the color of this beetle," said I. Then I formed a vision of the beetle with a beautiful metallic violet exoskeleton. I rubbed clay on the beetle, and soon after that I was gazing upon the exact creature I had imagined, a four-inch beetle of a lustrous and nearly luminous purple color. It was unlike any beetle I had seen before, and I was sure no such beetle had hitherto been discovered. This astonishing transformation brought forth words of amazement from the natives standing behind me.

The beetle seemed unaware that anything unusual had happened, and it continued picking its way through the living vines as it walked along the edge of the table. Occasionally it tipped its body headfirst over the edge before apparently deciding it did not want to fall off, after which it would pull itself back from the brink and continue on its original path.

An experiment then occurred to me that I had not thought of before. If the Lamotelokhai could put visions into my mind, perhaps it could influence the thoughts of other creatures as well. This time I simply spoke my request aloud.

"I wish to alter the way in which this beetle behaves," I said. "It seems to fear walking over the edge of the table. I wish for it no longer to fear this."

I reached out to apply another pinch of clay to the beetle's back, yet then I stopped, thinking that perhaps it was not necessary, as I had already applied the clay once. The creature continued walking, occasionally testing the table's edge and then pulling back, obviously unwilling to lose its footing and fall to the floor. Then, however, after several more attempts, it suddenly seemed to hold no fear. Without a moment's hesitation, it walked off the edge and plunged to the floor, landing upon its back. Unharmed, it used its large mandibles and slender legs to turn itself over. I placed it back upon the table, only to watch it fall to the floor again.

As I watched the beetle continue this behavior, I contemplated the implications, and again I was overcome with foreboding and dread. If it was such a simple matter to change the beetle's behavior, perhaps I could influence the thoughts and behaviors of any living creature, including men. Perhaps I could cure madness or intellectual deficiencies. However, perhaps I could also persuade men or women to carry out acts against their own will. I could scarcely imagine what might happen if the Lamotelokhai were to fall into the hands of a mad man, or perhaps just a man with lordly ambitions. My thoughts on this matter consistently led to my imagining undesirable consequences. It seemed that for every possible benefit of this clay, there were innumerable wicked deeds to be contemplated.

I wished to try many more experiments, but Sinanie was determined to limit the duration of each of my sessions with the Lamotelokhai. Consequently I was then taken to more of the village huts to continue learning about the daily life of these peculiar people. During the process I met several villagers for the first time, including yet another woman, only the fourth I had seen, although I had met at least twelve different men. It was interesting to learn more of the tribe's customs, but I could not prevent my thoughts from returning to the Lamotelokhai and all it could do.

Even now, as I sit alone in my hut, writing beside the open doorway to catch the last of the day's light, I can think of little else. There are no natives below my hut to prevent my leaving. I have food in my belly and water to drink. Although I have no civilized clothing, I now possess a gourd that covers my private organs, which somehow seems to place me at a level equal to the other men of the village. And I dare say that I am beginning to think of Sinanie and a few of the others as friends. I am in good health. In fact, I feel physically improved beyond any time of my previous life, no doubt due to the medicinal benefits of the Lamotelokhai. And there seems to be yet enough scientific questions to investigate to keep me busy and stimulated mentally for a very long time.

Although I do hope to see my beloved Lindsey again someday, presently my will to escape this village has dissolved.

13

MAY 5, 1868

It seems my wish for a peaceable existence will forever elude me, as today I was again a witness to murder. Penapul and a half dozen of his warriors attacked this village. They must have been hiding in the forest north of the village, perhaps waiting for any unsuspecting individual or small group to walk nearby. An opportunity came to them when three tribesmen, Korul, Ot, and Teatakan returned from a hunting excursion, unaware they were walking into an ambush.

I was with Matiinuo and Sinanie, learning about their process of making strong cord and rope from plant fibers, when we heard shouting. We quickly grabbed spears and joined the other tribesmen who were running to the scene of the disturbance. However, we were too late. Ot and Teatakan lay dead or injured upon the ground, and Korul was maimed and bleeding from numerous wounds. Penapul and his men saw us coming, and they gathered into a defensive line, brandishing spears and steel choppers that were red with fresh blood.

Sinanie, Matiinuo, and a dozen other tribesmen formed a

line, shoulder to shoulder, facing the Humboldt Bay men. I stood for a moment, frozen with indecision, but then I stepped up beside Sinanie and held my spear toward the attackers in the same manner as the others. I was keenly aware that I was defending the tribe that had held me as their captive. However, not only had I grown fond of them, but also they were the stewards of the Lamotelokhai, which I now understood to be of immeasurable importance.

Upon seeing me with his enemies, Penapul called out to me. "*Ané lai-m, Samuel! Nokhu ima-fon khüp Miok, Loo, Amborn.*"

"Penapul, a terrible thing has happened," I said in English. "Miok, Loo, and Amborn are dead. But you have taken your revenge. You must now leave this village, or you surely will be killed."

Of course my words were not understood. The men at my side began advancing, one step at a time, while repeatedly uttering loud grunts that were no doubt intended to intimidate Penapul and his men. To the side I saw Korul stagger and fall, finally succumbing to his grievous wounds. Matiinuo broke from our line, ran to Korul, and dragged his body back behind us. Matiinuo then shouted with rage at the attackers and rejoined our line of defense.

"You have killed three men!" I shouted to Penapul. "Justice has been wreaked. Please yield."

But my words were useless. Sinanie and the others rushed forward, leaving me standing alone, uncertain of what I should do. I was quite sure I would help Sinanie defend the village against an attack, but Penapul's men were now outnumbered, and it seemed they could do no more harm. At first I thought perhaps Sinanie's advance would serve the purpose of forcing Penapul's men to flee, but they did not retreat and were immediately overwhelmed by fifteen attackers.

In mere seconds the fighting was over. Four of Penapul's men lay writhing upon the ground, and the others had run away to save their own lives. I then watched with mortification as the four fallen invaders were stabbed repeatedly until they were most assuredly dead. This act of barbarism should not have shocked me so much, considering what I had previously seen these savages do. However, what I found to be so unsettling was the indifferent and apathetic manner in which they extinguished the lives of the helpless men, as if the task were no more significant than slapping bothersome flies.

When Sinanie and his fellow tribesmen were certain the men were dead and that Penapul and his warriors were truly gone, they turned their attention to their own fallen men. With scarcely a word spoken, they carried the bodies of Teatakan, Ot, and Korul to the hut where the Lamotelokhai was kept. They did not even check the men to see if they were still alive. With an ease of manner, as if they had done this many times before, they employed an elaborate technique of hoisting the men up using ropes that seemed to be there for that very purpose. When all three of the bodies were in the hut, I followed the remaining men up the ladder. At this point there were so many natives in the hut that I feared it might collapse under the weight, but it held fast. Three women were present, but they hid themselves from me by standing behind the men in such a way that I only occasionally saw portions of their faces, and I could not determine if they were the females I had seen before.

The three bodies were arranged beside the low table holding the Lamotelokhai. Matiinuo pulled a bit of clay from the large lump. He went to Ot's side, forced open the lid of one of the man's eyes, and rubbed the clay directly onto the eyeball. He then repeated this operation with Teatakan and Korul. This apparently concluded the treatment of these fallen men, as most of the natives then left the hut. Sinanie came to me and indicated that I should leave as well, and he followed me to the ground.

I said to him, *"Yekhené mbakha-mol-mo-dakhu khomilo?"*

MY TRANSLATION:
"Will the men die?"

SINANIE NODDED AT ME, indicating that he was impressed by my rapidly improving use of his language. He then began walking with me to my hut. He replied, *"Lamoda-Lamotelokhai. Béto-pé lép afü-ma-tél-e-kha menél khi-telo."*

MY TRANSLATION:
"They were touched by the Lamotelokhai. Afterward the very sick people become healthy."

IT THEN OCCURRED to me that his words for 'very sick' might have had a much broader definition than I had previously assumed, and that perhaps these natives did not even distinguish between 'very sick' and 'dead.' I attempted to form the correct words to inquire about this.

His answer was extensive and somewhat confusing. My interpretation, although perhaps imperfect, was that he believed that indeed there was no difference between 'very sick' and 'dead.' The Lamotelokhai could heal both of these conditions. However, he pointed out that there was a distinct difference between 'dead' (*khomilo*) and 'very dead' (*khomilo-ayan*).

I then asked what 'very dead' meant, and he explained that it took much work to make a man 'very dead.' It was necessary to pound, or stab, or cut the man's body until there was nothing remaining, at which point the clay of the Lamotelokhai could no longer make the man healthy again.

When we arrived at my hut, Sinanie left me alone. I walked north to again visit the site of the attack. The Humboldt Bay men still lay where they had been slaughtered, but they were now in an advanced state of decomposition, with nearly half of each body already turned to soil. This had to be the result of the natives putting portions of the Lamotelokhai upon the bodies, just as they had done to the bodies of poor Charles and my three boys. I found it unnerving that the same clay, from the same source, could somehow preserve life in one instance and destroy life in another. I returned to my hut to once again ponder the implications of the strange things I had learned.

I am apparently free to leave this village whenever I wish. However, I have determined the Lamotelokhai to be too important for me to leave now. In recent days I have learned much about it, not the least of which is that there may be no limits to the miracles it can perform. Instead, the limits exist only in my capacity to communicate clearly what I wish for it to do. Hence, there is much work yet for me to do here, and it is difficult to express how important I believe this work to be. It seems inevitable that this mysterious lump of clay will eventually be taken from Sinanie's tribe, and then, due to its extraordinary nature, it will find its way by trade or outright seizure into civilized society. This I have grown to fear above all things, as I can imagine the ways it will be used to further the power and wealth of the few, thus resulting in even greater suffering of the many. And very little effort is required to imagine far worse consequences.

Now I fear that Penapul will return, bringing with him more of his warriors and seeking further revenge. If he overcomes Sinanie's tribe, he will likely steal the Lamotelokhai and take it back to Humboldt Bay, thus commencing a sequence of events that will deliver it into the hands of more influential men.

To add to my fears, I had met no fewer than forty men when living with Penapul's tribe. Here in Sinanie's tribe I have seen only eighteen men, three of whom are now injured at the very least.

We are greatly outnumbered.

14

MAY 14, 1868

IN THE DAYS following the attack, there was much consternation among the villagers. This was the first time that *laléo* (the word for outsiders or strangers, particularly those of evil nature) had ever attempted to raid this village. Apparently, Sinanie and his fellow tribesmen had a habit of killing any hunting parties who happened to wander near the village, thus resulting in other tribes of the region altogether avoiding the area. This explained why Penapul had been happy to send Charles and I to collect in this place, and why he had wished for my three boys to return upon guiding us here. He had wished, as I had suspected, to be rid of us without risking the lives of the boys.

My command of the tribe's language had much improved by this time, and several days after the attack I suggested to Sinanie that the tribe move to a new location farther inland. He told me he would propose this possibility to Matiinuo, who was the tribal elder. In order to further expound upon the merits of this suggestion, I also explained that Humboldt Bay, due to its excellent quality, would attract more ships and would eventually become colonized. After I explained what the term "colonized" meant, this seemed to concern him, which was the result I desired. However, he explained that moving the village would require a great deal of effort, as new houses would have to be built and new hunting grounds established. In addition, they would likely have to fight and drive away another tribe whose territory they would have to claim as their own.

I then suggested they could go to Penapul's tribe and attempt to establish peaceful relations by offering gifts, or perhaps goods for trade. Sinanie seemed completely perplexed by this notion, and no amount of discussion could convince him that such a relationship between tribes could ever be possible.

Hence, as the days have passed, and as I have learned more about the habits of this tribe and the wonders of the Lamotelokhai, so have I kept my eyes on the dark shadows of the forest, fearful that Penapul will return with all of his warriors.

At this time I must conclude my writing, as I have exhausted the last pages of my notebook. In recent days, I have contemplated destroying this notebook, as it occurred to me that it might lead men with evil intentions directly to the Lamotelokhai. But I have decided that it is only a matter of time before civilized men, regardless of their moral character, discover the Lamotelokhai anyway. This notebook, therefore, might serve as a warning to those who would find and read it. I truly hope my words have adequately explained the importance and dangers of what has remained hidden here in the most remote jungle for such a long time.

15

MAY 21, 1868

I EXPLAINED to Sinanie my quandary regarding my shortage of pages on which to write. He then looked with only mild curiosity at my notebook. By all reckoning, this should have been a significant revelation for a savage who previously had never used written script as a means to communicate. As Sinanie's tribe had long ago forbidden direct engagement with the strange figures created by the Lamotelokhai, these figures were now little more to them than fanciful designs to be carved upon objects as ornamentation. As such, Sinanie may have considered my somewhat less-than-elegant handwriting to be rather crude attempts at decorative art. He nevertheless led me into the forest to show me a tree with loose bark that could be peeled off in large sheets. The backside of the bark was smooth and light in color, and would be suitable as paper. I thanked him prodigiously, to his amusement, and collected a pile of sheets. Later I trimmed them to the same size, dried them, and bound them together into a serviceable notebook using cord I had learned to make from plant fibers.

Upon the first pages of my new notebook I wish to

describe in some detail what I have most recently learned of my indigene hosts.

Notwithstanding the barbarous state of these natives' existence, I have witnessed various events and customs such that I am compelled to reconsider my original conclusions, leading me now to regard certain aspects of their culture with some esteem. In fact, I find it unavoidable to draw comparisons to the culture of the three-legged creatures that created the Lamotelokhai, whom I have seen in my visions to exist in a state of civilization that all societies should aspire to someday achieve.

As I have previously stated, it is my opinion, as it is the opinion of many learned men, that the highest state of civilization would afford equality to all individuals, both in wealth and social station. Remarkably, the two indigenous tribes I have lived among, but particularly Sinanie's tribe, seem to have achieved such equality. Admittedly, there is little or no wealth to speak of here, but each member of the tribe seems to have access to the same resources as all other members. Even the huts themselves are shared, as the natives move about and sleep in whichever hut is positioned most conveniently for the activities they are currently engaged in. If three men are preparing for a hunting excursion, they will gather their bows and spears and other supplies and sleep together in the hut nearest the direction they wish to embark upon the first light of morning. If several women wish to process raw sago into sago paste, they will gather the necessary ingredients in the hut where they have built drying shelves of clay, and there they will work and sleep until their task is complete. The resulting sago paste, as well as the meat procured by the hunters, is then made available to all members of the tribe, in whatever quantities they may need. When supplies run out,

Matiinuo gathers the tribe together to inform them that more is needed. At these gatherings, the villagers have been accustomed to render voluntary obedience, and typically there are adequate numbers of members who will engage themselves willingly in the needed tasks. Upon the rare occasion that all the villagers are unwilling due to being occupied in other tasks, Matiinuo, being the tribal elder, will simply assign the work to be done to those he wishes to do it. What I find to be most striking is that any or all members of the tribe who have the skill and inclination may participate in the requested tasks. The only exception to this that I have seen is hunting, which seems to be restricted to the men of the tribe.

Another example of the social equality of these people is the treatment of the three men attacked by Penapul's tribe. The wounds of Teatakan, Ot, and Korul were treated in the same way that any other members of the tribe would be treated. In addition to this, it seemed that all members of the tribe participated, or at least had the opportunity to participate, in administering care to these injured men.

This led me to inquire of Sinanie as to whether or not there were individuals of the tribe who were particularly skilled at healing, such as a shaman. His response indicated that there were indeed several men, including himself, and one woman, who were often consulted regarding such matters due to their knowledge and skills.

It is inevitable that, in an advancing society, specialization or division of labor will become essential, as advancing knowledge renders it impossible for one man to learn all the particulars of more than one or two specific fields of specialty. A barber learns the intricacies of the coiffeur's art in order to provide the latest styles of the culture in which he works. The factory worker learns to operate the specific machinery of his assigned station. The naturalist, such as myself, learns the taxonomy and physiology of the specific sorts of living things that inspire his interests, such as the mammalogist's inclination for beasts bearing fur.

But in the 'great' societies of the world, the vast majority of citizens have little choice in the occupation in which they specialize. This again is a result of the accumulation of wealth. The vast majority have little or no wealth and likewise little or no choice in their occupation. Those few who are fortunate to have wealth, myself included, may pursue whatever interests them. But in the tribe of the savage, where wealth is nonexistent, it seems that all men and women have the same opportunities to pursue whatever occupations or activities they may wish.

With such equality, the savage tribe does not know of wealth and poverty, education and ignorance, or master and servant. Most incitements to great crimes are thus lacking, and petty ones seem to be rare.

This, however, does not mean that in this village justice need never be administered, as I was witness to one such event. A tribesman by the name of Kaura was accused of invoking taboo by requesting of the Lamotelokhai certain personal benefits. Several tribesmen noticed that Kaura's physical features had somewhat changed, indicating that unfitting requests of the Lamotelokhai may have been made. Matiinuo himself came to fetch me to attend Kaura's inquest, as apparently this was yet another aspect of their customs they wished me to understand. I was taken to the hut of the Lamotelokhai, where about ten other men were gathered and seated on the floor. Two women were present as well, but they quickly left the hut upon seeing me arrive.

The inquest, or trial if it could be called that, was brief.

The men who were the accusers explained what they believed to be evidence of wrongdoing, primarily that Kaura's body had changed in certain ways. Kaura was then told to stand up, so that all could better see him. Even I could see that his arms were rather longer than one would expect. In fact, Kaura's general structure seemed to more resemble one of the great apes, such as the Orangutan, the great man-like ape of Borneo. This gave Kaura a rather alarming and powerful appearance, although his face had scarcely changed at all. There was much nodding of heads and words of agreement that some rule or law had been violated, and Kaura, apparently seeing that he had no choice, admitted to the infraction.

Being aware that these men were capable of barbarous acts of violence, I expected Kaura's punishment to involve such acts. However, instead he was simply told to make right what he had done wrong. As everyone in the hut watched, Kaura called forth the tree kangaroo, which seemed to always be somewhere nearby. Kaura employed the peculiar language of gesticulations to communicate with the creature, after which the tree kangaroo did the most peculiar thing. The creature responded to Kaura's gesticulations by scratching its own belly with its forepaws. Then, before my very own eyes, the skin of the abdomen gave way, splitting apart as one paw was inserted several inches into the abdominal cavity. Soon the paw was withdrawn, and upon it rested a small mass of bloody entrails. Apparently without thinking this to be the least bit strange, Kaura took the dripping mass from the tree kangaroo and ate it.

Notwithstanding my own bewilderment at such behavior, the natives seemed satisfied with this, and most of them rose to their feet and began leaving the hut. Apparently they believed justice to be done. I approached the tree kangaroo for closer inspection. There was no longer any sign upon its belly of the self-inflicted wound. Sinanie, Noadi, and several other natives remained in the hut, watching me. I then had a discussion with them in which I learned a great deal of new information. I have decided it best to write the particulars of this conversation just as it occurred, except that I will translate the natives' words to expedite the writing and reading of it.

"The *mbolop* (tree kangaroo) is unharmed," said I. "How is this possible?"

Sinanie replied, "The mbolop cannot be harmed. It is of the Lamotelokhai."

For a moment I assumed he must have meant that the tree kangaroo was protected by the medicine of the Lamotelokhai's clay, as were he and his fellow tribesmen. However, then I realized that he had used the word '*keliokhmo,*' which meant 'to make' or 'to come together from,' and that he was implying that the tree kangaroo was indeed made from the same clay that made up the Lamotelokhai.

"How did the mbolop come to be?" I asked.

Sinanie's answer was extensive. "The mbolop exists because Matiinuo requested it to be so. This was long ago, before other men came to this land, and our tribe was the only tribe here. Our tribe crossed the big water for many days to come here. Matiinuo found the Lamotelokhai, because it called to him in his dreams. The Lamotelokhai was near the water's edge. Matiinuo touched it, and he saw the *woliol* (figures) in his mind." Sinanie paused and pointed to the figures carved upon the gourd that covered his sexual organ. "After that, Matiinuo saw other great things in his mind, and he became an improved person. He suffered no more from *walukh* (general sickness, but also the suffering of old age). He knew then that the Lamotelokhai had magic power, and he took the others of the tribe to it, and the others became improved. Life was then very good for our tribe, and there was no walukh. However, one day, Matiinuo's brother, his name was Izack, went alone to the Lamotelokhai, and he talked to it. He asked for *lu gamo* (to ascend and become strong, or to become *very* improved). He then became strong. However, he became *lelül lokhul* (infected in the brain, perhaps meaning he became insane). Izack wanted to have the Lamotelokhai for himself. However, my tribe, we also wanted the Lamotelokhai. Izack was improved and strong. He attacked my tribe, which was his own tribe, and he killed men, women, and children. He used the magic power of the Lamotelokhai's clay to make them *khomilo-ayan* (very dead), and they could not be healed. But his brother Matiinuo went with more men and killed Izack. They beat him with clubs and beat him and beat him until he was khomilo-ayan. That is when Matiinuo and the others of my tribe declared that talking directly to the Lamotelokhai was to invoke taboo. Matiinuo made one last request directly to the Lamotelkhai. He asked it to make the tree kangaroo. Now we talk only to the tree kangaroo. The tree kangaroo knows what is taboo. That is how the tree kangaroo came to be. That is why the tree kangaroo cannot be harmed."

As Sinanie was explaining this, Noadi left the hut and soon returned with a white object in his hand. When Sinanie finished talking, Noadi handed the object to me. It was a very large tooth, more than four inches long, most likely from a crocodile. Upon its surface was etched in astounding detail a scene of bloodshed, in which bodies of men were strewn about on the ground, some of them missing arms or legs. In the center of all of this stood a creature that at first I thought was a man, but upon closer inspection more resembled a great ape, its arms elongated, with long, curved fingers. This creature was Izack, having been transformed by the power of the Lamotelokhai. And in some ways Izack resembled Kaura, although Kaura's transformation had not yet been as extreme as this. At first I wondered why both men would request to be changed in such a similar way. Then it occurred to me that, in this place of dense tropical jungle, this was the most desirable body form, as it would allow them to move about in the trees with great agility. As I gazed at the creature etched in the tooth, standing over his maimed victims, an uneasy chill overcame me, as if I were gazing upon the devil himself.

When I handed the tooth back to Noadi, he left the hut again, as if he were resolute in returning the tooth immediately to its rightful place.

I took a moment to ponder all of this new information. "When you captured me and killed my companions, you applied clay from the Lamotelokhai to their bodies and our belongings."

Sinanie nodded. "The clay helps the bodies and the belongings return to the soil of the forest."

This explained how our sack of supplies disintegrated before our very eyes. "How is it that you can do such a thing without talking to the Lamotelokhai?" said I.

Sinanie smiled at me as if he were talking to a schoolboy. "Each of the men in our tribe carries with him a skin pouch, and in it he keeps clay of the Lamotelokhai. This clay can be used for different purposes, and we do not have to talk to the Lamotelokhai. The clay knows what purpose we intend when we apply it to something."

Notwithstanding the peculiar nature of this explanation, I was still curious about the tribe's notions of justice. "Kaura talked directly to the Lamotelokhai," said I. "And he asked it to make him very strong. That is why he was accused."

Sinanie said, "That is correct. Kaura agreed to *fudamo* (to repay or repent), which he did. Now he will not become lelül lokhul and kill us."

I asked, "How do you trust that he will do what you have told him to do?"

Sinanie looked at the other men beside him, and they smiled as if I had asked a question with an obvious answer. "We witnessed his fudamo. You yourself witnessed it."

Apparently they could not imagine, or perhaps it was indeed impossible, that Kaura could have deceived them.

I then said, "I talk to the Lamotelokhai, and you don't accuse me. Why?"

Sinanie answered, "You are *laléo* (an outsider). We have always known an outsider would come who could talk to the Lamotelokhai in different ways. The Lamotelokhai told us this long ago. This outsider, when he comes he will take the Lamotelokhai away, and then true Lamotelokhai will occur."

This confused me. "What does 'true Lamotelokhai' mean?"

"The world will end," he said. "The world will turn upside down and it will end. That is the meaning of the word Lamotelokhai. That is why it is the name we have given to the magic clay."

"Do you mean that *your* world will end, or do you mean that the entire world will end?" Finding the correct words to ask this question was difficult, and perhaps I was unsuccessful because the natives seemed unable to understand. Or perhaps they simply did not perceive any distinction between these two notions.

My waning confidence in using their language was

uncompensated by any great success in asking my next few questions, which regarded their laws. This was perhaps due in part to the fact that they had no written language by which to record specific laws in any permanent form. Therefore their laws, such as the prohibition of talking directly to the Lamotelokhai, were subject to varying interpretations by each individual. However, upon further inquiry, I determined that there was more to it than simple interpretation. They were confounded by the notion of having specific laws to be followed by all people under all circumstances. How, they inquired, could one administer justice to a man without considering the man's situation and the events that led to his behavior? After considerable discussion, I came to understand that these natives did not live within the confines of specific and rigid laws. Instead, they were subject to a natural sense of what was fair and just in any situation, as determined by public opinion and with regard to the rights of their fellow tribesmen. Perhaps this is a sense that is inherent in every race of man, but the power to adhere to it becomes lost in more densely populated and 'civilized' communities.

What I found to be most striking was the manner in which they administered justice. I said to them, "You did not harm Kaura, as I thought you might." I was not aware of a word for 'punish,' as perhaps they did not have one. "What will prevent him from again directly talking to the Lamotelokhai?"

Sinanie answered, "Kaura did not harm us. Why would we harm him?"

"If you harmed him," said I, "he would not do it again, as he would fear being harmed again."

They dismissed this notion as absurd. I attempted to explain that in some communities, including my own city of

London, those who failed to obey the laws were often punished harshly, sometimes even maimed or executed in painful ways. Sinanie and his companions were aghast and could not understand why these people were not simply told to make right whatever they had done wrong. If a man had taken something, for example, why would he not simply be told to return it? I said that sometimes the crime was very serious, such as murder. In this case, they said, why would he not be told to increase his efforts in order to provide whatever assistance to the tribe that the murdered man could no longer provide?

"But you have said that Matiinuo's brother, Izack, was killed when he murdered members of your tribe," said I.

Sinanie answered, "Izack intended to continue killing. We stopped him."

After pondering these notions for a moment, I said, "When you encountered me, you murdered my companions. And then you maimed me without mercy. Why?"

Sinanie said, "We did what was needed. We kill outsiders so they will not take the Lamotelokhai from us. We did not kill you because the mbolop told us you might be the man who will come to talk to the Lamotelokhai, the man who will better understand it and will take it away."

"Am I that man?"

"We are not yet certain."

"Why did you maim me?"

"We did what was needed. You intended to run away. We stopped you."

This confirmed my impression that these natives did not comprehend the notion of punishment. They simply did what they felt was necessary, and being savages, that did not preclude maiming and killing. But as I considered their response to what I had told them regarding justice and punishment in London, it occurred to me that they might consider *me* to be the savage. This was a rather dismal thought, so I decided to pursue other questions.

"I have seen no children in your village. Why?"

"We have children when we need them," Sinanie replied. "At this time we do not need children."

"I do not understand. Your tribe will die if you do not have children."

Again the natives smiled as if this were something I should already understand. Another tribesman who was present, a man I had not previously spoken to, by the name of Tinal, answered this question. "If we had children always, there would be too many people in our tribe. Our tribe is the correct size."

"Perhaps your tribe should be larger," said I. "If the Humboldt Bay tribe returns with all their men, you will be too few."

Sinanie said, "That tribe believes they have killed Teatakan, Ot, and Korul. They will not return. Our tribe is the correct size."

"How do you know your tribe is the correct size?" I asked.

The men looked at each other again, although this time they did not smile. The answer that followed confounded me. It continued to inundate my thoughts even into the dark of night, and later I would lie in my hut, unable to sleep as I pondered its meaning.

Sinanie said, "Our tribe is *wakhatum* for the Lamotelokhai (wakhatum refers to folktales, or stories, or knowledge, in this case referring to those who keep the stories and knowledge). Our tribe is the correct size for this. The Lamotelokhai contains much wakhatum (in this case the meaning is closer to 'knowledge'). It is knowledge that will turn the world upside down, which will be Lamotelokhai (the end of the world). The knowledge is very important, and so the Lamotelokhai has put some of the knowledge into each member of our tribe. Our tribe is the correct size for the knowledge. If we had more men and women, there would be no more knowledge for them to carry, and they would have no purpose. We each carry the knowledge given to us, and there is no more knowledge."

I spent several moments pondering what he had said. Then I asked, "Why did the Lamotelokhai put knowledge into each of you?" I asked.

"The knowledge is important. It is our purpose."

"Do you know what the knowledge is?"

Sinanie smiled. "We know the knowledge is important. It is very much. It is too much for us to know."

I attempted to ask him how it could be possible to carry knowledge and at the same time not know what the knowledge was, but asking this seemed to be beyond my ability, as it resulted only in frowns and shaking of heads. Therefore, I decided to pursue this specific matter at a later time, after having time to formulate proper questions. I returned to a previous question still on my mind.

"What if one of you is killed and becomes khomilo-ayan (very dead)? What becomes of the knowledge?"

Tinal answered this question. "That is the time when one of our women will have a child, so that our tribe will be the correct size. The child will then be given the knowledge previously carried by the khomilo-ayan."

Notwithstanding the bewildering nature of this answer and the myriads of new questions it created, I instead asked a simple question. "And how long ago was the last time that the tribe had to have a child?"

Once again the men smiled, and Tinal replied, "A very long time."

I was curious as to precisely how long this was, but I had already determined that these natives had only a rudimentary sense of mathematics and did not possess the means to express large numbers with any exactness. Instead, they expressed the passing of time with regard to past events. As I pondered this, something Sinanie had said came back to beleaguer my thoughts.

"You have said that Matiinuo found the Lamotelokhai when your tribe came to this land. Matiinuo is the elder of your tribe, correct?"

Sinanie said, "Yes, Matiinuo is the oldest. He lived when our tribe came across the big water. The rest of us came into the world after Matiinuo found the Lamotelokhai."

I took a moment to devise a way to ask my next question. Finally, I said, "I would like to know how long Matiinuo has lived. What can you tell me to help me understand?"

The men considered this, and then Sinanie replied, "When Matiinuo found the Lamotelokhai, he became improved, and he no longer suffered from walukh. Before that, he was a normal man. Normal men do not live long, and so he was very young when he found the Lamotelokhai. Matiinuo is now the only member of our tribe who existed when our tribe came over the big water. The others have died, long ago. I came into the world soon after Matiinuo found the Lamotelokhai, so I am almost as old as Matiinuo. There were no other tribes in this land when I was a child, and for many days after that. The animals were different then. Some men of our tribe were killed and eaten by crocodiles with teeth like this." He held his fingers apart to show that the teeth were as large as the one Noadi had shown me, with its carved scene of Izack and his murdered victims. Sinanie continued, "We hunted the *wolaup*, which was a slow creature with a delicious, fleshy snout and two very large front teeth. The wolaup had the weight of four men. We hunted the *ndewé*, a wallaby that stood taller than you, Samuel, and had the weight of two men. And then other tribes came over the big water, and they also hunted these animals, until these animals were gone. We had to kill many men so that they would not take the Lamotelokhai's magic. Finally the other men stopped coming near our village. Those are events that have happened since Matiinuo came into this world."

Due to the tendency of savage people to express the past in the form of myths and fantastical stories, I could hardly say which portions of Sinanie's answer were factual. However, if indeed these men had lived when such beasts roamed the forests of New Guinea, I could scarcely imagine a lifetime of such a span of time. Such changes would no doubt take hundreds of years, perhaps thousands, or perhaps even many thousands. Had I not already seen impossible things made entirely possible by the clay of the Lamotelokhai, I would have dismissed this notion altogether.

Now I do not know what to believe.

———————

ONE OTHER RECENT event is worthy of describing before the day's light fades. Yesterday I had the opportunity to accompany three tribesmen on a hunting excursion. This was the first time I had departed from the village for any substantial distance, but Sinanie and Matiinuo were unconcerned that I might run away. They likely knew as well as I that I could not return to the Humboldt Bay tribe, and I certainly was not capable of living by my wits alone in the wilderness.

The three natives I accompanied were Teatakan, Ot, and Korul, the very men who had been injured, and perhaps even killed, by Penapul's men. They had recovered fully from the attack and now bore only faint scars that appeared to have healed for many months. I had the impression that these three men loved hunting above all other things, and in fact they provided the majority of animal meat eaten by the tribe.

In a matter of only a few hours after leaving the village, the hunters had killed three bandicoots. These were of the same large type my assistant Charles had shot many days ago, before he was murdered. The bandicoots were peculiarly docile, even to the moment of their death by arrow or spear, as if they were the most stupid of domesticated livestock, existing solely for slaughter and consumption by men. Upon asking the hunters about this, I learned that this behavior was not a phenomenon of nature, but was indeed due to these bandi-coots being somewhat domesticated by the tribe. Rather than confining the creatures to pens near the village, in which they would have to be cared for and fed, the beasts were allowed to freely roam the forest of the region. Then hunters, such as my three companions for the day, could go in search of them when the village's dwindling supply of meat required it. This I found to be notable. Other Papuan tribes were known to have domesticated dogs for help with hunting, but I was quite sure none were known to have domesticated animals of any type for the purpose of harvesting.

Immediately after killing each of the bandicoots, the men butchered them using the same sharpened bamboo wedges they had once used to sever my heel tendons so that I would not run away. Notwithstanding my distressingly perfect memory of this barbarous act, I was impressed by their skilled and efficient manner of removing the meat and skin. They expertly cut the skin from the body in one large piece, removed the meat and other edible organs, placed these upon the skin, and then gathered up the edges of the skin and tied it off, thus creating a sack to be easily carried.

Teatakan told me they would typically hunt these bandicoots until each hunter had a skin sack full of meat to carry back to the village. However, on this occasion, since I was there to carry one of the sacks, they became quite excited for the opportunity to pursue an additional creature, a cassowary. I told them that my assistant Charles had killed a cassowary, and that I had found the meat to be delicious. Upon hearing this, the hunters laughed as if I had intended for my story to be amusing. When I asked why this was funny, they indicated that they did not believe this to be possible. They explained that the cassowary was the most elusive of all game and could be killed only by the most skilled hunters, most certainly not by a man such as myself, who had no hunting experience. Rifles were apparently unknown to them, and I made no further attempt to explain. I became quite curious to see how, without a gun, they could kill such a large and swift creature. They referred to their hunting technique, as well as to the few men capable of achieving it, as *kayareumala*. *Kayarie* was the name given to the cassowary, and *mala* signified making war, which further indicated that they considered the hunting of cassowaries to be a more serious venture than the hunting of other game.

We walked perhaps a mile to a place where cassowaries were known to frequent. Korul and Ot went off to find supplies that would be needed for kayareumala. Teatakan stayed with me and began gathering grass fibers and rolling them together between his hands, creating thin and flexible cord. As he did this I asked him to tell me more about kayareumala. The following is his response, to the best of my ability to translate.

"The kayarie (cassowary) is the spirit of a woman, and all kayarie originated in the world of women. I, and other hunters, we are from the world of men. In order to catch a cassowary, we must pass into the world of women. To do this, we must achieve *yikeulaka*, which means to be possessed by the spirit of a cassowary. When we enter the world of women, we must be very careful, as women have wisdom that is different from the wisdom of men. We must be careful, or we will be tricked and harmed, perhaps killed. The first of us to achieve yikeulaka will be the one to try to catch a cassowary. The others will drive the cassowary to him. Then we must leave the world of women and not return to it for many days. If we have success and catch a cassowary, we will carry the meat and feathers to the village. The others will eat the meat and adorn themselves with the feathers. But we, the kayareumala, must never eat the meat or we will not again be allowed to enter the world of women. And we must not lay with a woman for many days, or we will not again be allowed to enter the world of women."

This explanation served to heighten my desire to witness the process. Before long, Korul and Ot returned with the needed supplies, which included leaves of a female pandanus, three pandanus flower heads, each about the size of a large mango, and a handful of small brown mushrooms. I observed with some curiosity as the men fashioned the pandanus leaves and flower heads into cassowary masks, held together by the fiber cords Teatakan had made. These masks, which were striking in appearance and ingenious in design, featured beaks made from the long, rigid pandanus leaves, and the pithy flower heads were arranged to represent the cassowary's large horny calque or helmet upon the top of the head.

The hunters then divided the small pile of mushrooms and ate them, after which they began to dance, mimicking the bird in its search for food among the trees. This went on for some time, and I began to wonder if they had any intentions at all of hunting cassowaries. No less than an hour passed as they danced about, their movements becoming ever more tipsy and haphazard. I began to suspect that the mushrooms the men had consumed had some intoxicating effect upon them.

At last Ot stopped dancing, and his body seized with violent trembling. This, I was later told, indicated that he was the first of the three men to achieve yikeulaka. Apparently he was now possessed by a cassowary's spirit and could enter the world of women. When Teatakan and Korul saw Ot's trembling state, they rushed to him and supported him by grasping his arms. Soon the trembling subsided, and Teatakan told me —much to my relief—that they were now ready to hunt the cassowary.

We placed the three skin sacks of bandicoot meat in the forked trunk of a tree to keep them safe, and we put all of the hunting weapons on the ground below, with the exception of Ot's bow and one arrow. Still adorned with their cassowary masks, the hunters led as I followed, and we slowly and silently made our way up the densely-forested slope of a rather substantial hill. Finally, when the ground was becoming level near the hill's summit, the hunters stopped and stood very still. I then saw ahead of us a large cassowary. The bird, apparently unaware or uncaring of our presence, was searching for food. Its motions reminded me of the men's dance. We carefully retreated down the slope until we were out of the bird's sight. Without a word spoken, Teatakan walked up the hill to the left, Korul to the right. Ot, his eyes peaking out from his mask, nocked his arrow and positioned himself behind a thick tree. He waved his hand at me, indicating that I should move further down the hill, which I did and then stationed myself behind a tree. I watched as Ot waited for Teatakan and Korul to circle behind the bird from both sides, presumably to drive it straight down the slope. This seemed to me to be an unlikely consequence, as the bird could just as easily run off in any other direction.

However, I was soon surprised to see the cassowary walking unhurriedly down the slope, rather than running with great rapidity as I had expected. Teatakan and Korul followed slowly on either side, far enough behind so as to avoid driving it to complete panic. When the bird would drift to the right, Korul, who was on the left, would stop, and Teatakan would continue moving, gently forcing the bird back to the left. In this way they were able to drive the cassowary within range of Ot's bow. At the critical moment, Ot, remaining mostly behind the tree, bent his bow and shot the cassowary.

Before Ot had released his arrow, I had thought that this unusual cassowary hunt would be nearly finished soon after shooting the bird. I was quite mistaken. As I later learned, an arrow could rarely kill an animal as large as a cassowary, at least not instantly, which was why bows were seldom used in fighting other tribes. Instead, the arrow's purpose was to cause the bird to have a brief moment of surprise and confusion. At the precise moment Ot's arrow was released, he dropped his bow and ran with full rapidity directly at the bird. The arrow pierced the cassowary, startling it for the briefest moment, and then the bird began running. However, Ot was so close behind the arrow that the bird had insufficient time to gain full stride. Ot leaped headlong for it and managed to grasp one of its legs. The cassowary, weighing more than a hundred pounds, turned upon its attacker with the fury of an injured beast.

The cassowary is known to be a dangerous bird, with a powerful beak and toes armed with long, curved claws, which could inflict serious injury to anyone so unfortunate as to be attacked. Ot was instantly engaged in a vicious fight to the death, while Teatakan and Korul, and even myself, were still too far away to lend immediate assistance. I arrived at Ot's side before the others, and by this time he had managed to straddle the bird and grasp its slender neck in his hands to choke it. I attempted to grasp its thrashing legs but could not do so without great risk of encountering the formidable claws. Suddenly, and with the great desperation seen only in a dying beast, the bird twisted itself in such a way that Ot tumbled off to the side. Then the bird's legs both caught him in the abdomen and sliced downward with a revolting sound. Ot released the bird's neck, and it immediately rose to its feet and ran away, disappearing into the trees. At that moment Teatakan and Korul arrived, and they gazed down with surprising calm at their wounded companion.

Teatakan was the first to take action. He rolled Ot onto his back. I then saw that the worst of Ot's wounds would have been, under any normal circumstances, quite fatal. It was an immense and dreadful gash from his rib cage, through his abdomen and groin, and down his right leg nearly to the knee. The gash lay open in such a way that his intestines could be clearly seen, some of which had been torn open, their contents strewn about within his abdominal cavity. I could not imagine

how the Lamotelokhai could heal such a grievous wound, even
if it were possible to carry Ot to the village in a timely fashion.

While Korul and I attempted to hold the gash closed to
prevent spilling of the entrails, Teatakan opened the small
pouch hanging from a cord around his neck. From the pouch,
he brought forth upon his fingers a lump of clay, presumably
from the Lamotelokhai, and spread it upon the torn skin. Such
a small amount of the clay seemed to me to be an absurdly
trivial measure when considering the wound's magnitude, and
I thought that Ot would most assuredly expire from excessive
bleeding before any medicinal benefits could occur. Teatakan
then joined us in attempting to hold the wound closed, and for
some minutes we continued this, the only sounds being Ot's
miserable cries from below and the singing of honeyeaters
from the trees above.

Finally, it seemed that Ot's skin was beginning to fasten
itself together. We pulled away our hands, and the gash
remained closed. Korul stayed with Ot while Teatakan and I
gathered enough long sago leaves to build a rough shelter for
the night. Rain began falling as darkness set in, and we spent
the night under the shelter. Although I could sleep scarcely
more than a few minutes at a time, I must say that I felt oddly
as if I belonged there in those miserable circumstances, with
savage hunters who desired to treat me as one of their own.

By the first light of morning, Ot was able to walk, although
only slowly. We returned to the tree where we had left the
three sacks of bandicoot meat and found that one of them had
been torn open and partially eaten by some unknown arboreal
creature. We began walking with the remaining meat back to
the village, and soon the hunters were laughing and discussing
how they might tell the tale of the hunt to the other villagers.
It was as if they had experienced such things on many occa-

sions before. By the time we neared the village, Ot was able to walk just as swiftly as any of us.

However, this fateful excursion held one last distressing surprise. Just as we approached the village edge, we came upon two natives. We apparently startled them, as upon hearing us approach from behind, they turned and ran. For a brief moment I caught a glimpse of their faces.

The two natives were men I knew to be from Penapul's tribe at Humboldt Bay.

16

MAY 24, 1868

I AM BEGINNING to believe a great burden is upon me, one that I am not qualified nor inclined to bear. The natives have suggested that I may be the man they have waited for, the man who would speak to the Lamotelokhai in new ways and would somehow take it away from the village. As they tell it, the Lamotelokhai has informed them that the arrival of such a man is inevitable. Perhaps I am that man, and perhaps I am not, but with each passing day my fear of the Lamotelokhai's power grows ever stronger.

For the first time since I was brought to this village, I have a strong desire for a stiff glass of brandy, or perhaps an entire bottle, as it would help to becalm my mind so that I may write these words with objectivity and then sleep without troubling dreams. Today I experienced an event that may forever haunt my soul. I considered foregoing the distress of writing its particulars in this notebook, but as I have already taken such pains to include all relevant information here, I feel obligated to describe it. If the Lamotelokhai should ever make its way to civilization, by my hand or by another's, this notebook may provide a warning. Or perhaps at the very least it will provide important insight.

I awoke this morning in a state of melancholy. In my new life here, I am comforted by the respectful way the indigenes have now decided to treat me and by the scientific pursuit of a better understanding of the Lamotelokhai, a worthy and stimulating endeavor. Yet not a day passes in which I do not long for the company of old friends and family, and particularly of my betrothed, Lindsey, whom I fear I may never see again.

In recent days the villagers have stopped taking me to the Lamotelokhai's hut for my experiments. Instead, Matiinuo has told me I may visit it whenever I wish, although he did stipulate that at least one tribesman was to be there to witness what might occur. Hence, this morning, after pacing about my hut in an unsuccessful attempt to distract my thoughts from distressing subjects, I found Sinanie and went to the Lamotelokhai. Upon placing my hands on the lump of clay, I had no particular requests in mind, so I simply spoke aloud to it in English, as if it were a human being.

"I am confounded by my situation," said I. "I feel that I can no longer presume to know what is right and wrong, what is benevolent and malicious. However, I do know that I wish to see Lindsey, although I am uncertain she would favor the man I am becoming. I wish to place my hand upon her cheek, and to tell her of the wondrous things I have seen." I pondered what I had just said, and I nearly laughed at the absurdity of speaking in such a way to a lump of clay, regardless of where it had come from or who had created it.

In hindsight, I now know that I should steadfastly avoid the Lamotelokhai's hut when my mood is desperate. However, at the time I could not recognize my own mistake. I said to the clay, "Ignore what I have previously asked of you. I wish to be with my beloved Lindsey. If you never grant another request, please at least consider this one."

And then it was too late. I no longer in the Lamotelokhai's hut. Instead I was standing in the drawing room of my Georgian house in Fitzrovia, London. It was just as I remembered it. I inhaled the fragrance of wallflowers and moss roses, as several bunches had been arranged elegantly in vases upon my piano. The chairs and tables were arranged just as I had left them. Suddenly I heard a voice behind me.

"Samuel, what a pleasant surprise!"

I turned about, and there before me was Lindsey. Her chestnut-colored hair was braided and pinned into a low bun at the back of her neck. She was wearing my favorite skirt and bodice with sleeves, both of soft lavender dye and simple embroidery, and neither with the elaborately trimmed confections of high fashion.

For a moment, I naturally assumed the Lamotelokhai had placed another vision into my mind. However, in all previous visions, I had been merely an observer, in which my presence was of no consequence, nor was I even detected by those I observed. Now, though, in this vision, Lindsey gazed directly at me, awaiting my response.

"Lindsey," I said, stammering. "It is you, as if I had never departed."

"Yes, Samuel, it is I, and I am so happy you are here with me now."

She walked gracefully to me and placed a hand upon my cheek. I felt the warmth of it and smelled clove perfume on her wrist. Fearing that she might vanish if I were to move, I carefully raised my hand and placed it on her cheek. At that moment, I knew she was real. As I gazed at her face, my eyes were drawn to my own hand against her pale and clean skin.

My fingernails were uncut, and the skin was darkened by many weeks of unwashed dirt and healed scars. I looked down at my own body and was suddenly quite mortified, as I was still completely naked but for the filthy gourd tightly fitted upon my sexual organs. I withdrew my hand and stepped away from her.

"I am so sorry for my appalling appearance. You must think I have become a savage."

She smiled. "Whatever do you mean, my love? You look perfectly dapper and trim, as you always do."

Before she even finished speaking, I felt a change come over my entire body. I looked down again and saw that I was now wearing my favorite waistcoat over the yellow linen shirt Lindsey had given me. Below that were tweed trousers and my waxed calf oxfords. I had nearly forgotten the sensation of clothing against my skin, and I found it to be rather confining, although certainly more appropriate for the situation. I then realized that I had forgotten all of this was merely a vision, so pleased was I in again seeing my betrothed.

"Lindsey," said I, "I do not know if it is truly you, or if you are nothing more than a lovely vision of my mind's making."

She smiled again. "Do you like the flowers? I bought them from the flowergirl we often see on Whitfield Street."

"They are lovely," I said.

"She told me her name is Hattie. Did you know that?"

Again I was already forgetting that this situation was not real. "No, I did not know her name. The poor girl seems very dear, though."

She walked to the piano and pressed only one key, D sharp, as she inhaled the fragrance of the flowers. She held her finger on the key until the note faded to silence. "I bought two bunches, but I paid her for four," she said.

At that moment I convinced myself I was indeed talking to Lindsey, rather than an apparition. After all, if she were a figment of my own making, how could she know the flower-girl's name?

"It is so good to be here with you, Lindsey," I said. "My expedition has not gone well. I fear my collection has been lost, although I hardly had the opportunity to accumulate anything more than the most common birds and insects. And Charles, my assistant, has been killed. I will have to report this news to his family."

She turned to face me. "That is dreadful, the poor man. And I am sorry to hear about your collection. Perhaps you can begin again."

I stepped closer to her, and this time, rather than touching her face, I put my arms around her and embraced her tightly. Again I smelled her clove perfume. I spoke tenderly near her ear. "I do not know how this is possible, but I have been given the opportunity to speak to you, although I now exist in a pitiable state in the darkest jungle on the opposite side of the world. It is an opportunity such as no man has ever had before, yet I find it difficult to find the right words to say to you."

She whispered back to me, "You are here, Samuel. That is all that matters."

And with those words I became enraptured and set aside all of my doubts. Perhaps later, I thought, I could decide what to tell her and what horrid particulars to keep contained within my own memory. For the moment, all that mattered was that I was with her, and I continued embracing her for a good many minutes as we spoke in whispers about matters of little consequence. I was happier than I had felt in many weeks. However, this was not destined to last.

When I finally released my embrace and pulled away, I

happened to glance downward just as the collar of her bodice lifted away from her neck, and through the gap I had an unobstructed view down her front. But instead of gazing upon her undergarment and pale skin, I saw a strange blackness. I witnessed it only briefly, just long enough to determine that it was not at all what the cloth's thickness and the angle of the window's light should have revealed to me. It was strangely alarming to behold, and my doubts again began to grow.

I gazed into her eyes and saw nothing peculiar there. But a seed of doubt and contempt had been planted in my mind.

"Lindsey," said I, "what has happened since I departed from London? My parents, are they well?"

She smiled at this. "Of course they are well. They speak of you often."

"And what news of my brother, Owen?"

Her smile nearly turned into a laugh. "You're trying to trick me. I know you don't have a brother."

She was correct on that matter, and the trick had failed. I then asked, "What news can you tell me of Prime Minister Disraeli's cabinet? I imagine he has appointed men to all stations by now, has he not?"

Lindsey gazed at me for a moment, but her smile did not fade. Finally, she laughed. "I'm sure you would rather tell me of your adventures."

I did not relent. "Please, I wish to hear of the cabinet and parliament. Tell me what has transpired. I insist."

She laughed again. "I would rather—"

I interrupted her. "I insist, Lindsey!"

Never before had I spoken to her in such a manner, but this did not dampen her mood. In fact, she laughed yet again. This supported my growing suspicion that she was no more than a fantastical vision, constructed from what I already knew of her, as I had never before seen her become angry. I was incensed by the possibility that she was not real, and rather than simply appreciating this gift the Lamotelokhai had given me, I became even more determined to drive her to anger. I wanted so badly for her to be real that I concluded that her anger would prove she was capable of something more than my own memories of her. Hence, I then said something that would infuriate any lady of civilized society.

"I wish for you to remove your bodice and skirt," I said. "Please do it immediately." Upon uttering these words, I felt great shame, as I would never typically say such a thing to a member of the fair sex. I began to apologize, but it was too late.

Still laughing, Lindsey removed her bodice and sleeves. I attempted to turn my eyes away, but then I could not, as the horror of what I saw before me caused me to stumble backwards and nearly fall to the floor. Rather than a typical cotton undergarment, as one would expect, below Lindsey's shoulders was blackness such as I can scarcely describe. It was not the darkness of black cloth, or even of black velvet, but rather a blackness so absolute that I knew there was simply nothing there at all. She then removed her skirt, revealing more of the same infinite blackness.

She took a step closer, and I backed away, quite horrified. Her head and shoulders were just before me, as were her hands, wrists, feet, and ankles. All else was simply an absence of anything at all. I could see only that which was in my memory. As was proper for a gentleman, I had never seen more of Lindsey than what I could see at that moment.

She spoke as she came even closer. "Samuel, let us talk about pleasant things. Have you met interesting people on your journey?"

I cried out and covered my eyes, as I could endure no more of this vision.

When I lowered my hands and opened my eyes, I was once again in the hut of the Lamotelokhai. Sinanie was still there, frowning and watching me with interest. In an unpleasant state of distress, I told Sinanie that I intended no further experiments with the Lamotelokhai, and I hastily left the hut.

After careful consideration, I have decided I must tell the Lamotelokhai to never again, under any circumstances, put visions into my mind, even if I request it. In fact, I may even ask if it can make me forget it is possible to speak to it at all. It is indeed a most powerful substance, but I have come to believe it is as dangerous as it is fascinating, and that it will bring great suffering to the world. Its rightful place is here, hidden deep in the wilderness.

17

MAY 26, 1868

I WISH to tell the events of today exactly as they happened, as I am in no condition to express meaningful comments regarding their implications. Perhaps in the coming days I can reflect on these events with some measure of objectivity.

This morning I had resolved to visit the Lamotelokhai to demand that it never again put visions of any kind into my mind, which again I had determined to be necessary for my sanity. I fetched Sinanie, and scarcely had we climbed the ladder to the Lamotelokhai's hut when we heard a great commotion to the north. Immediately I assumed the worst, and when I saw villagers carrying spears and running toward the commotion, I knew my assumption to be correct. The village was again being attacked.

Sinanie and I each were handed spears by the other men as we ran to defend the village. When we reached the source of the commotion, my worst fears were realized. The Humboldt Bay tribe had returned, this time with many more men. Although I did not see Penapul, at least thirty-five men and boys from his village stood shoulder to shoulder, advancing steadily as they grunted in unison. Including myself, fewer than fifteen defenders opposed them. Teatakan, Ot, and Korul were gone on a hunting excursion, and two of our men were already lying injured or dead on the ground. We were outnumbered by at least twenty men.

The line of attackers, armed with spears and steel choppers, continued advancing one step at a time, and we had no choice but to yield. At this rate, we would soon be forced out of the village, and Penapul's men would then overrun the huts and take from them whatever they wished, including the Lamotelokhai.

Sinanie and Ahea were to my right. Matiinuo and ten other villagers were to my left. I looked at Matiinuo, and for the first time I saw fear in his eyes. I had learned enough about these natives to know that they did not fear death. The one thing they truly feared was failing in what they believed to be their primary purpose.

Unexpectedly, another commotion arose behind us. It was a woman's voice, a sound I had never once heard while living in this village. I turned around to see a woman tumble from the door of a hut and fall fifteen feet to the ground. A man from Penapul's tribe began climbing down from the hut after her, but he appeared to be injured. The woman attempted to get up but could not. Suddenly, two other men were upon her, and they drove their spears through her body. I stared at her murderers, shocked from witnessing their brutal act. I then saw that one of them was Penapul.

I cried out, "Matiinuo, they are attacking from behind!" In my haste, I failed to speak this in his language, but it was of no consequence because at that moment the line of invading attackers yelled fiercely and rushed forward, stabbing and chopping madly.

Never before had I been faced with such a violent onslaught, and having had no experience whatsoever with fighting, I was nearly paralyzed with distress. Coming directly for me with his chopper was a man I had met at Humboldt Bay, by the name of Nabul. He had been kind to me then, and we had never quarreled, but now he clearly intended to slice me to bits. The only advantage I had was the length of my spear compared to that of his chopper, and so I thrust it at him to hold him beyond effective chopping range. As he swung his chopper at my spear again and again, apparently intending to hack it to a shorter length, several men beside me succumbed and fell. The attackers from each end of the advancing line then began circling behind us. They would soon overwhelm us, as no man could simultaneously fight enemies before and behind him.

Sinanie cried out, *"Keliokmo dimo!"* Immediately the ten or so men who were still able to fight gathered together into a circle, facing outward. I recognized what they were attempting and inserted myself into their formation. This quick and coordinated action seemed to cause our attackers to pause. For a moment, all was strangely quiet and still.

Our situation seemed to be hopeless, and during this brief respite, I determined that these men had to be stopped at any cost. They could not be allowed to take the Lamotelokhai, as this would most assuredly have dreadful consequences.

"I must go to the Lamotelokhai's hut," I said to Sinanie. Again I neglected to use his language, as I was too distressed to form the correct words. I hoped that the word Lamotelokhai was sufficient to convey my meaning.

I gazed directly at the attacker before me. "Nabul," I said

to him, "I am sorry." I then took two steps forward and thrust my spear at his face. He stepped back, hacking at my weapon and forcing it to miss. Just as the men on either side of Nabul turned their weapons on me, the two men at my sides stepped out to engage them, giving me the opportunity to drive Nabul back even farther. He tried desperately to counteract my thrusts, but I did not relent, and my spear punctured his cheek and glanced off his teeth. He retreated, holding a hand over his torn face, and I took this opportunity to run, leaving my companions behind to fend for themselves. As I ran, I saw Penapul and two other men attacking another woman, but rather than stopping to help her, I continued running.

Much to my relief, Penapul's warriors had not yet entered the Lamotelokhai's hut. I climbed the ladder hastily, kneeled before the lump of clay, and put my hands upon it. As I did this I heard shouts of anger and distress from the fighting below.

"I beg for your help," said I. "Penapul has come for revenge. The men and women of this tribe are all going to perish if I do not do something. I know you have put your knowledge into these people, hence they are important to you, as they are to me. They are being murdered, all of them."

At that moment I was nearly overcome by the most dreadful visions in my mind, appearing at a bewildering rate. There was fighting and killing, with much bloodshed.

"Stop, I beg you," I cried. My thoughts were already jumbled. I had seen too much violence and had no desire to witness more, nor did I want to have a hand in murdering more people. "I do not wish to kill Penapul and his men," I said. "Nor do I wish for Matiinuo's men to kill them. But they must be stopped! Can you help?"

Between my hands, a bulge on the clay began to rise. I

could think of no other purpose for this except that it was forming there for me to take. So I pulled loose the handful of clay, descended the ladder, and ran. The woman I had failed to help lay dead upon the ground as I passed.

Penapul and the other men who had attacked from behind had joined the main group and were moments away from completely overwhelming Sinanie's remaining men. Only seven of our tribe remained. Matiinuo and Noadi were among the bodies strewn about at the feet of those still standing. When I saw this, great fury boiled within me such that my thoughts of a peaceable outcome turned to thoughts of revenge. I ran directly at Penapul, pulled loose a portion of the clay in my hand, and threw it. The clay struck him in the chest. He paused and wiped some of it off. He gazed at the clay in his hand for a moment and then looked at me and laughed, perhaps assuming I had gone mad. He turned his attention back to the battle. I then approached his men as closely as I dared and threw bits of the clay at them until I had hit every Humboldt Bay tribesman. As I was holding no weapon and was throwing what appeared to be harmless clay, the warriors ignored me and continued their onslaught. By the time I had finished this, only four of my companions remained standing.

I did not know what effect the clay might have on the attacking men, or if it would have any at all. Another of Matiinuo's tribe fell, leaving only Sinanie and two others, Ahea and a man named Faül.

"Penapul!" I cried out.

By that time only a half dozen of Penapul's men were active in the fight, circling the three survivors and waiting for an easy opportunity for a fatal chop or thrust. The others were standing back, watching. Penapul turned and looked at me.

His face was injured in two places, but this did not prevent him from forming a smile.

Although I hadn't the opportunity to become proficient with Penapul's language, my greatly improved memory served me well at this time. "You have murdered my friends," I said to him, using his language as best I could. "These people are now dead. Those still living are too few to be a threat to you. Let them live and they will go far away to make a new village."

By my reckoning, Penapul likely had no understanding of the notion of *khomilo-ayan*, or 'very dead.' If he would spare only one or two of us, we could apply the clay of the Lamotelokhai to heal the injured and even the recently dead.

Penapul said something to his men, and they halted their attack. It was clear that Sinanie and the two others were utterly exhausted. They could hardly hold their spears up, and it would take little effort for Penapul's warriors to dispatch them. Penapul and three others approached me, and I backed away, which caused them to circle me to prevent my escape. I began to think that the Lamotelokhai's clay was harmless to them, and that my life would soon end.

Penapul spoke to me, and the following is my attempt to translate.

"We have feared this tribe for a long time. Our men came here to hunt but did not come back. Hunters from other tribes came here, but they were not seen again. Amborn, Miok, and Loo came here with you, and they did not come back. Now this tribe will be dead, and we will not fear them again."

"You can go home now," I said in his language. "Now they are not to be feared."

Penapul smiled again. "We will complete our task, and then we will go home. We will take the heads with us. The skulls will hang in our houses, and we will look at them often and tell stories of this day."

I looked at him with renewed alarm. If they beheaded the bodies, this would most assuredly thwart the Lamotelokhai's healing powers. And if they killed every last one of us, there would be no one to apply the healing clay anyway. Suddenly I realized all would be lost.

Penapul handed his spear to the man next to him and took the man's chopper. He then approached me. I glanced about, but his warriors had surrounded me. Penapul stopped when he was close enough to strike me down. He slapped the flat edge of the long and bloody blade against his hand several times, as if to taunt me in my final moments.

The events that occurred next are nearly beyond my capacity and will to describe, but I believe that they should be told and known.

Penapul began speaking to me, but then he stopped after uttering only the first word. For a moment he seemed confused. He then grasped the chopper with both his hands and pressed the tip of the blade to his own throat. I thought perhaps he was taunting me yet again, but suddenly he threw himself upon the ground. This action drove the blade through his throat and it emerged from the back of his neck. I stared down at Penapul with great shock as his body immediately began floundering about with violent spasms, causing his own men and myself to step back to avoid being thrashed by his arms and legs.

I looked up at Penapul's men, and they seemed to be as shocked by this as I was. But then one of them dropped his spear to the ground and began screaming. He simply stood with his arms at his sides, crying out with such force that he sounded more like a wild beast than a human being.

Beside the screaming man, another warrior threw his spear aside. He then ran with all his strength toward the nearest tree. At the last moment before hitting it, he bent at the waist so that his head hit the tree, instantly breaking his neck. He fell to the ground and did not move again.

Another man turned his spear upon himself. He thrust the spear's point into his ribs, and when he could push it no further, he placed the blunt end of it against the ground and leaned into it with all of his weight until blood began oozing from his mouth. He then fell to the ground to die.

During all these horrible actions, the screaming man's wailings seemed to grow ever more desperate.

Another man dropped to his hands and knees, and with great strength he began throwing his own head downward, repeatedly striking his face against the ground, transforming it into a ghastly pulp—but still he did not stop.

By this time, the general mass of the Humboldt Bay men had been thrown into a state of utter panic. Many of them tried to run away, but before they had run even a dozen steps they abandoned the attempt and engaged in the most unthinkable suicidal acts. I saw a man force his hand into his mouth and down his throat with such force that it killed him. Another man went to the tree where his companion had broken his own neck, stepped upon the man's body, climbed the tree, and then threw himself to the ground. Most of the men, however, turned their own weapons against themselves.

When at least half of the men had died, I could endure the sight no longer, and I turned away so I could not see it and held my hands to my ears to deaden the cries of the man who still stood screaming with his arms at his sides. Oddly, in my mind I could think only of the stag beetle I had once seen walking fearlessly off the edge of a table.

Suddenly it occurred to me that perhaps I could stop this savage mayhem. I could run to the Lamotelokhai and request another handful of clay that I could apply to the surviving men to prevent their suicides. Instead, I simply stood with my eyes closed and ears covered, unwilling to save them—unwilling to allow the survivors to return to their village, only to attack us again at some future time.

When the man who had been screaming finally stopped, I turned around. He had collapsed and was now apparently dead. He had screamed with such vigor that blood had flowed from his eyes, and he had spewed forth bits of his throat and lungs.

So blunted were my senses by the horror of what I had done that it took some time for me to realize that Sinanie, Ahea, and Faül were the only men, other than me, who were still standing.

Sinanie's eyes were wide as he spoke to me. *"Samuel, yekhené-pan-to ülmo. Gekhené khokhukh-tebo semail-e-khén kül. Gu laléo-lu. Kho funé yanop golole-té-do yalén, yanop khedi-fa-fon-dakhu."*

My translation:

"Samuel, they killed themselves. Your anger is like the anger of a crocodile. You are a powerful spirit. All the people should be afraid, because you will exterminate all the people."

Sinanie, Ahea, and Faül then turned their attention to their dead and injured companions. There were too many for so few men to carry, so they instead went to fetch the Lamotelokhai.

I still had not moved from the place where I stood, and I felt quite unable to do so. Instead, I simply gazed at the carnage around me. Every last man and boy from Humboldt Bay had been exterminated.

18

JUNE 1, 1868

I have occupied no small measure of my time in recent days by contemplating what it is that distinguishes a civilized society from a barbarous one. I am sure there are many opinions on this. Some may believe it is industry and wealth. Others may feel that it is acquisition of lands. Perhaps it is a robust system of government, of administering justice, and of national education. Or perhaps it is a rich culture of artistic and scientific achievements. Or it is all of these things combined. But I have come to believe that above all these things there is one quality that most distinguishes the civilized man from the savage. That single quality is compassion.

Compassion is what motivates us to respond to the suffering of others by helping them. It is important to distinguish between compassion and sympathy. Whereas sympathy implies a general concern for others, it does not imply acting upon that concern. Men who have compassion do indeed feel sympathy, but they go beyond this sympathy and actually behave in ways that benefit the welfare of others.

In the great 'civilized' societies of the world, such as

London, there is an astounding preponderance of suffering among the populace, and there is no shortage of sympathy. Sympathy in fact seems even to be fashionable among the wealthy. However, sympathy does not alleviate the suffering—compassion does. Hence, having contemplated this endlessly, I have determined that a general inclination for compassion is the one last achievement that lay beyond the reach of great civilizations.

There is yet another conclusion I have made. In order for a man to be compassionate, he must have the capacity and will to imagine himself in the body of another human being, so that he may understand the other's thoughts and feelings. This can be achieved only if he is able to believe that he and the other human being are similar, perhaps even equal. A wealthy European man may have little difficulty feeling compassion for another wealthy European man. However, that same man may fail to feel compassion for others if he believes they are fundamentally different from himself, due perhaps to their lack of wealth, poor breeding, lower station in life, or physiognomy and skin color. It seems to me, therefore, that this belief that others are different, perhaps inferior, is exactly what prevents men from feeling compassion, and therefore it is what prevents societies from becoming truly civilized.

I have come from the world's greatest city, but am I a civilized man? Due to my actions, and subsequently to my inaction, forty-four men and boys suffered most excruciating deaths. If I had felt some measure of compassion for them, would I not have attempted to stop the slaughter? If they had been men more like me, perhaps white men who spoke English, would I have still wished them to die?

I attempted to convince myself that their deaths were

beyond my control. My fateful request to the Lamotelokhai had been as follows: "I do not wish to kill Penapul's men. Nor do I wish for Matiinuo's men to kill them. But they must be stopped."

I have endlessly considered these words, and it seems they were interpreted literally, yet incorrectly. I failed to state clearly that I wished for the men to be stopped without the men actually dying. One could argue that this was an honest mistake.

However, that does not change the fact that, upon witnessing my friends being stabbed and chopped, I desired to kill Penapul's men. My anger was such that I wished for all of them to die, and when I had the opportunity to prevent this, I took no action.

When it was over, after we had treated our fallen men and women with the clay of the Lamotelokhai, I considered the possibility of also treating the bodies of the Humboldt Bay men.

It seemed that it might be the right thing to do, but again I did not act on this thought.

WHAT IS the purpose of the Lamotelokhai? This is another question I have pondered in recent days. Perhaps it was created and sent here in order to determine which societies are truly civilized and which are comprised of savages. Perhaps, in fact, it was sent here to rid the world of populations that fail to acquire certain qualities deemed important by its creators, such as compassion. What I find distressing about this notion is that Matiinuo's tribe has lived with the Lamotelokhai for hundreds of years, perhaps even thousands.

However, I fear that if the Lamotelokhai were taken to London, its ill-intentioned use could bring a quick and disastrous end to that great society.

On the other hand, perhaps the Lamotelokhai's purpose is merely to share the knowledge and power of its three-legged creators. If that is so, then it seems my responsibility should be to take it out of this remote corner of the world and put it into the possession of those who would better learn from it.

Sinanie and his tribe, all of whom have recovered from their injuries or deaths, now seem convinced that I am the man who is to take the Lamotelokhai away. They have told me this, although they have hardly spoken to me otherwise since the massacre. They have made no further attempts to teach me about their culture, as if they fear me and are simply waiting for me to take the Lamotelokhai and leave.

However, this I must never do, as I believe it to be improbable that the Lamotelokhai could be used with any measure of compassion. Even in the hands of learned and well-intentioned men, the Lamotelokhai could be used with dreadful results. In the hands of less honorable men, the results would be unthinkable. Hence, I will endeavor to convince the natives to continue hiding the Lamotelokhai from the rest of the world. So important is this to me that I will remain here and will use whatever influence the tribe has granted me to make it so.

I wish to tell of one more event, which happened today, and then I will wrap this notebook, along with my others, in the dry bark of the *yakhuo* tree to preserve it, and I will put it in a safe place, as I have no further intentions of writing upon its pages. I have found that writing in my notebook has become an invitation to melancholy. As it is unlikely that I will leave this place any time soon, writing frequently of my daily experiences only serves to remind me of my loved ones and the civilization I may never see again. I will add more words to these pages only when significant events occur to warrant it. If you should find yourself in possession of my notebooks, please take heed of the warnings I have provided herein.

Today I visited the hut of the Lamotelokhai for the first time since the massacre. Sinanie and Matiinuo both insisted on accompanying me there. I had decided that I must overcome my fear of it, as there was still much to learn.

Upon placing my hands on the clay, I hesitated, as I was not certain of how to make the request I had so carefully considered, nor was I certain that it was a good idea.

I spoke aloud and in English. "Lamotelokhai, I am not the man I once thought myself to be. I have done much thinking recently of such notions as compassion, sympathy, and peaceable intentions. I believe your creators possess such qualities beyond what I am capable of."

I glanced at Matiinuo and Sinanie before stating my request. "I would like to be improved," I said to the lump of clay. "Not my body, but my mind, and only with respect to these qualities. I wish to be the type of man your creators can respect, the type of man they would consider to be worthy of the knowledge they have endeavored to share. Can you help me with this?"

Then, before I could decide against it, I pulled loose some of the clay, placed it in my mouth, and swallowed it. Matiinuo and Sinanie shifted about on their feet and spoke softly to each other.

Matiinuo then said, *"Samuel, gekhené mbakha mo-mba-té?"*

My translation:
"Samuel, what have you done?"

I spoke to them in their language. "Do not be concerned. I have asked to be improved, but not in a way that might cause me to become *lelül lokhul* and harm your tribe."

They did not appear to be comforted by this explanation. However, it was done, and I had no inclination to undo it. I then picked up a hollow gourd I had brought with me. Crawling about in the gourd was a large orb-weaving spider I had captured. It had occurred to me that the silk of such a spider could be useful for many purposes, particularly if I could employ the Lamotelokhai's help to make the silk stronger, and perhaps to make the spider larger so that it could produce more of it.

But I must resist the temptation to describe the particulars of this, as I have vowed to stop writing in this notebook.

It has now been a good many hours since I asked the Lamotelokhai to improve me, but I feel no different than I felt before.

19

APRIL 24, 1944

THE GIFT of perfect memory was among the first gifts bestowed upon me by the Lamotelokhai seventy-six years ago. This faculty, of course, has been beneficial to me in my attempts to elucidate a better understanding of the Lamotelokhai, as well as in other smaller matters, such as keeping record of the precise year and date during my prolonged existence. However, it is also, in some respects, a curse upon me. Given such an extent of time, most men would gradually forget the faces and words of their loved ones. In every day that passes, though, I see the faces and hear the words spoken long ago by Lindsey and my mother and father, as if I had been with them only moments before. This makes it rather difficult to leave the past behind.

It is significant that seventy-six years have passed without the Lamotelokhai being discovered and taken to civilization. There was a time, particularly after I had realized my body had stopped aging, in which I believed that after this many years I would myself have taken the Lamotelokhai away from this village. Surely, I once presumed, mankind would progress in his social evolution such that a general sense of compassion and peaceable intentions would be achieved. However, it seems this presumption was terribly naive.

This brings me to the reason I have uncovered this notebook to once again write upon its pages. Someday, whether I live to see it or not, the Lamotelokhai will indeed be found by outsiders. When that day comes, I wish for my notebooks to be found as well, particularly if I am no longer alive to provide cautionary counsel to those who might need it. I want the world to know why I, Samuel Thaddeus Inwood, have made such efforts to delay the Lamotelokhai's discovery.

I have brought forth my notebook in order to describe events of the last several weeks, as these events have reaffirmed my conviction that the only safe place for the Lamotelokhai is here, hidden in the darkest jungle.

Beginning about two years ago, it became evident that endeavors of colonization and industry were taking place to the north, perhaps at Humboldt Bay. I occasionally could hear the low rumblings of some unknown and massive machinery, and a great many flying vessels would pass over us high above the trees. Imaginative men had long foretold of such winged machines, but never had I believed that they would fly with such rapidity and thunderous noise.

I became concerned that all of this industrious activity to the north might result in men venturing inland and perhaps discovering our village, but for two years the only evidence of their existence was the aforementioned disturbances.

However, nearly a month ago, the situation changed. Early on the morning of March 30, the ground began trembling from some massive and frightening disturbance to the north. I thought perhaps this was an earthquake, but the thunder and tremors of it continued for five days, after which all fell silent. During these five days we saw more flying vessels pass above us than I had ever imagined possible.

The area remained relatively quiet for more than two weeks after that. However, on April 19, a most disturbing thing happened. It occurred when I was on a hunting excursion with Teatakan, Ot, and Korul, an activity for which I had developed some fascination. We were east of the village in search of bandicoots, which seemed to have become somewhat scarce. Ot was the first to detect something out of the ordinary. It was a foul smell, perhaps that of a dead beast of some kind. We followed the smell several hundred yards to its source, and what I saw there will no doubt haunt my thoughts forever. Scattered about, sitting up against the trunks of trees or lying upon the ground, were the bodies of eleven men.

The men appeared to be of Japanese descent, or perhaps they were from Singapore. They seemed to be soldiers, as they all wore similar olive-green uniforms, although these were torn and terribly soiled from the most grievous cases of dysentery imaginable. Dysentery, in fact, was what appeared to have killed these men. Scattered about among the bodies were rifles of an unusual design, dome-shaped helmets of steel, and tall boots that had been discarded, no doubt due to swelled and fevered feet. It appeared that the men had brought with them no food or water, nor any other supplies.

Why would these soldiers venture so far into the wilderness without adequate supplies and medicines? Perhaps they had set out on a short excursion and had become lost, but it seemed more likely they had been forced to flee into the jungle and had no opportunity to gather what was needed.

As we looked upon this tragic scene, one of the men suddenly moved. He opened his eyes, and with obvious difficulty he focused his gaze upon us. I kneeled in front of him, but I had no water to offer, which is what he needed most, as dysentery drains every drop from the body.

The man then spoke to me. "*Koroshite kudasai. Watashi ga hazukashimete imasu.*"

I could not understand his words, but I was reasonably certain they were Japanese. I turned to my companions and spoke to them in their language. "We can help this man. He does not deserve to die in such a terrible way."

All three of them frowned, but Teatakan was the one to speak. "These men have travelled too close to our village. We must leave him to die. He is weak and will soon die. These men will then return to the soil and to their ancestors, as they should."

This was the response I had expected, and I knew it would be unlikely I could convince them to change their minds. For a moment I considered telling them that this man could possibly be the one they had waited for, the man who might speak to the Lamotelokhai in new ways and take it away. As I pondered this I gazed at the man, and then at his uniform, and then at the helmet and rifle that lay at his side. He reached for the weapon but was too weak to move it once it was in his grasp. I then decided to keep the notion to myself.

Korul set his bow on the ground and then held his spear with both hands, ready to thrust it. He said, "If you wish this man to die quickly, I will kill him."

I shifted my position to shield the dying man. "Do not kill him," I said.

Korul nodded and lowered his spear. "Come, Samuel, we will continue hunting. The man will soon die."

"You go," said I. "I will be just behind you. I wish to talk to this man. When I finish, I will call out to you if I cannot see where you are."

The three hunters agreed to this, and they continued walking east. I turned my attention back to the Japanese man.

"I wish I could speak to you in your language," I said. "There is so very much I could tell you."

The man's eyes were still upon me, but it seemed that he was unable or unwilling to speak.

I turned to look for Teatakan, Ot, and Korul, but the dense forest had already hidden them. I then pulled out the skin pouch I kept in the pocket of my waistcloth. With my finger I dug a small lump of clay from the pouch. I wiped it on the man's lips, and he swallowed it immediately, perhaps assuming it was food.

"I do not know what brought you to this place," I said to him. "But I do hope you find peace in whatever place you may go to next." I placed my hand upon my chest. "Samuel," I said. "Samuel Inwood."

I did not expect him to reply to this, so I returned my pouch to its pocket and began to stand up.

Then he did speak, although with obvious difficulty. "Iwataro. Iwataro Hayashi."

"I wish you Godspeed, Iwataro," I said to him.

As there was little more I could do, I then left him and his dead companions.

———

THE NEXT DAY I decided to travel north to Humboldt Bay in order to witness with my own eyes what was occurring there. Sinanie agreed to accompany me, and we departed the following morning with ample time to travel more than half the distance before nightfall. We arrived at Humboldt Bay on April 22. From my time spent with Penapul's tribe many years ago, I

knew of an area without trees upon the hill on the west side of
the bay that afforded an unobscured view. However, long
before we reached the hill's summit, Sinanie nearly convinced
me to turn back, as the air was filled with thunderous eruptions
so forceful that the hillside itself shook beneath our feet.
Having travelled so far to see what was causing these noises, I
was reluctant to retreat, and so we soon arrived at the open
view upon the summit. Before us was a scene so dreadful that
we simply stared at the bay without speaking for some minutes.

Humboldt Bay was filled with war ships. There were
dozens of them. The greatest of them were far larger than the
grand steamship *Deccan* that had carried me from England to
Singapore. Mounted upon these enormous ships of metal
were canons, which were the source of all of the thunderous
destruction. The canons fired repeatedly at the shore, sending
streaks of fire to destroy everything before them and filling the
sky above the bay with clouds of dark smoke. So violent were
the explosions upon the shore that it seemed impossible that
any man, beast, or plant there could still be living. If Penapul's
village had ever managed to rebuild its population following
the loss of its boys and men, they almost certainly could not
exist after this indescribable destruction.

Among the larger ships were smaller ones that appeared
to be completely loaded with men, and these vessels made
their way directly toward the beach. As I watched, one of
these ships ran right up onto the beach, where its load of
soldiers swarmed onto the shore amidst smoke and firing of
guns.

When I turned to look to the west, I saw great columns of
black smoke rising in the distance. It was as if the entire
northern coast of New Guinea were being attacked and

destroyed by the unimaginable power of these machines of war. Never before had I witnessed anything like it, and I hoped to never see such violence again.

Without a word spoken, Sinanie and I turned away and began our journey back to the village.

PERHAPS SOMEDAY I will be judged harshly for my actions. Perhaps those judging me will argue that the knowledge and power of the Lamotelokhai could have been used to prevent such lamentable warfare. How could this be, though, when such murderous intentions exist in the minds of men? How could such a war be ended or prevented? Would the people in possession of the Lamotelokhai use its powers to make all their enemies suddenly complacent and agreeable? If so, is it morally justifiable to forcibly alter the thoughts in the minds of other men? And where would that lead us to next?

Or perhaps the country in possession of the Lamotelokhai could bring about peace by simply exterminating its enemies? If so, I can tell you that I have seen such a solution with my own eyes, and it does not bring the peace and comfort of mind that you might wish for.

Perhaps you might argue that the Lamotelokhai's power could be used to provide every country with all the resources and wealth its people may desire, thus eliminating any want for war. But where do the desires of men end? Rarely do they end with accumulated resources and wealth. Instead, men then wish for power. They wish to own all of the lands of the earth, and even then their desires do not stop. Hence, the final result would still be war, but in this case it would be war between countries possessing unlimited resources. Such a war is frightening to contemplate.

Perhaps you might argue that I am simplifying this matter to the point of distortion, and that the greatest minds of the world will surely devise ways in which the Lamotelokhai may be used to bring about peace. If so, you may be correct, but I have had seventy-six years to ponder this, and I have significant doubts, which in the last few days have been confirmed. The world's greatest minds were apparently not able to prevent the war that is now taking place, and I believe I know why. It is because, as great as the world's societies may have become, they have still not achieved one very important characteristic: a general inclination for compassion.

Hence, I have convinced Matiinuo, Sinanie, and the others of the tribe to move the village far inland, to a place so remote that outsiders will not find it for many years to come. I will use the Lamotelokhai's help in concealing the village so that it will not be seen by men in flying vessels above, nor by occasional wandering hunters or explorers below. Sinanie and I have devised a plan for constructing huts high in the tallest of trees. Rather than being supported by poles, which are easily seen from the ground, these huts will hang from the trees themselves.

I do not know for how long we will manage to remain hidden, but I hope for many years. If you are reading these words, the Lamotelokhai has at last been discovered by outsiders, in which case you should pray to God for the wisdom and compassion required to use it safely. However, even this act is likely to be found wanting, as the Lamotelokhai's power seems to be independent of the gods of men.

We must all become improved.

THERE'S MORE TO THIS STORY

Is Samuel Inwood still alive?

Yes, and if you *really* want your mind to be blown, read more about Samuel and his impact on the world in the novels **Diffusion**, **Infusion**, and **Profusion**, as well as the novella **Blue Arrow**.

For more information on these novels, as well as updates about new releases and exclusive promotions, visit my website:

http://www.stancsmith.com

And be sure to check out my **Bridgers series**, as well as my **Across Horizons series**!

AUTHOR'S NOTES

I thoroughly enjoyed researching and writing **Savage**. Perhaps some of you have questions about the story. I tried to anticipate some of your questions, and I've answered them below. These are in no particular order, and they may not cover everything you're curious about, but if you're at all interested, here you go.

The Foreword of this book is written by Peter Wooley. Who the heck is Peter Wooley? Peter was the first outsider (besides Samuel) to come into contact with the Lamotelokhai. This happened when Peter went on an overly ambitious solo expedition to Irian Jaya in 1978. By the way, in Samuel's time, the Indonesian province of Papua was known as Dutch New Guinea. In 1978, it was known as Irian Jaya. In 2002 it was renamed as Papua. Anyway, back to Peter Wooley. Peter eventually played an important role in preparing the world for what he (and Samuel) thought was inevitable—the day when the Lamotelokhai would be revealed to the rest of the world.

If you want to read Peter's fascinating story of what happened to him after he encountered the Lamotelokhai, check out my novella **Blue Arrow**. This story is told by Peter's remarkable wife Rose. Also, Peter becomes an important character in the books of the **Diffusion** series.

Why does this book have so many old-fashioned words and phrases? Well, Samuel wrote these journal entries in 1868. This was the style of writing (and speaking) of people of Samuel's social standing at that time. How do I know this? I read a number of books written at that time. The most influential of these was Alfred Wallace's *The Malay Archipelago*, published in 1869. As you probably know, Alfred Wallace is a famous naturalist, a contemporary of Charles Darwin, and he even plays a role in **Savage** because he provided Samuel with valuable advice. Samuel was so inspired by Wallace's collecting trips that he decided to journey to Dutch New Guinea for his own collecting trip.

Samuel seems kind of racist and condescending to indigenous people. Was this really the way people thought in 1868? The books that I read, including Wallace's book, indicate that Samuel's attitudes were in line with those of other well-educated scientists, and probably far more progressive than many of the other people of that time. By our standards today, Samuel's attitudes would be considered inappropriate and offensive. It is important to consider, however, how Samuel's attitudes and ideas change during his harrowing experience. He becomes a very different man, and he ultimately admits that we all must become improved.

How much of this story is based on actual historical and scientific facts? As I'm sure you know, Samuel, Charles, Sinanie's tribe, and the Lamotelokhai are fictional. The names of Penapul and his tribemates are fictional, although there was a similar tribe living on Humboldt Bay, as described by the captain of the Hester Helena (which was a real ship). As for everything else, I tried to make the details as accurate as possible. Among other things, this includes the physical appearance of native Papuans (as described by Alfred Wallace), the descriptions of the ships and locations Samuel encountered during his travel from England to Dutch New Guinea, the Papuans using bird of paradise skins as items of commerce, all the birds, insects, and mammals mentioned in the book, building a hut to live in among a Papuan tribe, the strange ritual of Teatakan, Ot, and Korul as they hunted for the cassowary (including the mythology and mushroom consumption), and the horrifying destruction that took place in the area of Humboldt Bay in April of 1944 (the Battle of Hollandia, in which Allied Forces forced the Japanese to flee).

Why was Samuel still alive in 1944, which is 76 years after his last journal entry? Samuel was treated with the clay-like substance of the Lamotelokhai. The Lamotelokhai, as you know, was created by an alien civilization and is capable of repairing damaged biological tissue. This is why Samuel's horrendous injuries inflicted by Sinanie and his tribemates healed almost overnight.

Because it can repair biological tissue, the Lamotelokhai's clay can prevent aging. Anyone treated with the clay will not die of old age. They can still die from a violent accident, though, particularly if there is not a supply of Lamotelokhai clay handy to repair any injuries that are too massive for the limited supply of clay particles that remain inside the person's body indefinitely.

It's important to understand that the Lamotelokhai clay can also kill (basically, it can do almost anything). What the clay does depends on the intent of the the person applying it. If the person applying the clay wants it to kill someone, it will. If the person applying the clay wants it to decompose something (like a dead body, or any other object), it will quickly turn the object into soil. If the person applying the clay wants it to make someone obey every order, no matter how cruel or outrageous, that will be the result. Do you see why Samuel gradually realized how dangerous the Lamotelokhai might be?

Did the Lamotelokhai really bring back to life some of those tribesmen who were killed in battle? It is easy to underestimate the Lamotelokhai's capabilities. The Lamotelokhai's 'clay' is so good at what it does that it can even repair someone who has been killed, as long as they haven't been dead for more than a few minutes. This is why the tribe has different names for death: *khomilo* means 'dead,' and *khomilo-ayan* means 'very dead.' To make a person khomilo-ayan, one would have to literally mash the body into an unrecognizable pulp, which would be impossible for the Lamotelokhai to repair.

Matiinuo is the oldest member of his tribe. How old is he? We don't know exactly how old he is. Samuel was told, however, that Matiinuo was among the very first humans to arrive on the great island of New Guinea. Samuel didn't know this at the time, but today we know that archaeological evidence indicates that humans first arrived on New Guinea somewhere between 42,000 and 60,000 years ago. So, we can assume Matiinuo is at least 42,000 years old, and perhaps much older. Matiinuo did not encounter the Lamotelokhai until he arrived on New Guinea, so he probably was less than forty or fifty years old at the time (I'm guessing that the average life span of the people of that area that long ago was forty to fifty years). It's possible that Matiinuo may have died from numerous accidents during that vast amount of time, but obviously he was briefly *khomilo* instead of permanently *khomilo-ayan*.

Will Samuel live forever? Forever is a long time. But, like Matiinuo and his tribemates, Samuel could live thousands of years, as long as he isn't violently killed in a situation where the clay of the Lamotelohkai cannot repair his body.

Is there more to Samuel's story? Yes, absolutely! The **Diffusion** series (**Diffusion**, **Infusion**, and **Profusion**) takes place about 160 years after Samuel arrived in Dutch New Guinea. As you know, **Savage** is in the form of Samuel's field notebook, making it a rather unusual book to read. The **Diffusion** series is in a different style—fast-paced adventure with plenty of surprises and mind-bending twists. Many reviewers say that the series is unlike any science fiction they've ever read before. Check it out!

What's this **Diffusion** *series all about?* Many years after Samuel has been lost and forgotten, two teachers take a group of teens on a spectacular field trip to the Indonesian province of Papua. In the midst of social unrest, they are forced to evacuate. Tragically, something mysterious happens to their plane, and they end up stranded in one of the most inaccessible wilderness areas on Earth, which happens to be near the location of Sinanie's hidden village. Strange things begin to happen. Horrifying things. Wonderful things. The Lamotelokhai can make the world a better place, but it can also destroy everything. Either way, the world will never be the same. If you think the Lamotelokhai must always be in the form of a lump of clay, think again.

Was the Lamotelokhai actually from a distant alien civilization? Yes. This is not a secret. The Lamotelokhai tries to make this clear to everyone who comes in contact with it. It does this by inserting visions into people's heads while they are sleeping, as it did with Samuel. These visions show the astounding home world of the beings that created the Lamotelokhai (they also created thousands of other objects just like the Lamotelokhai). The Lamotelokhai points out to Samuel that its creators are likely long extinct. Why? Because it has been a very, very long time since the Lamotelkhai was launched into space. There is no way for the Lamotelokhai to know for sure because it's not possible to communicate with beings who are thousands of light years away (faster-than-light travel and communication are fiction, not reality).

Why did this alien civilization create and send out thousands of entities like the Lamotelokhai? This is an excellent question. The short answer: these beings wanted to have an impact on other civilizations. The question is, was their intent friendly, or was it diabolical? The long answer: well, the long answer requires three full-length books to describe. Fortunately, those books are readily available. They are titled **Diffusion**, **Infu-**

sion, and **Profusion**. I'm pretty sure you're going to like the long answer.

What was going on in Humboldt Bay on April 22, 1944? Was that something that really happened? Indeed it is. The Battle of Hollandia started on April 22 and lasted six days. This, of course, was in World War II. The Japanese had built a base with three airfields near Humboldt Bay. On the western shore of Humboldt Bay was a town called Hollandia, where 11,000 Japanese men were stationed. In the weeks leading up to April 22, multiple air raids by Allied forces had destroyed many of the Japanese aircraft (over 300 were destroyed). The assault on Humboldt Bay, which included numerous amphibious landings supported by relentless heavy naval bombardment, was met with little resistance from the Japanese. This was the horrifying sight Samuel and Sinanie witnessed. The Japanese were forced to flee into the jungle. 3,300 Japanese were killed in the attack, and 7,000 fled into the wilderness, most of them attempting to make it 145 miles west to the next Japanese base. Astoundingly, only 500 of these 7,000 men survived the ordeal. This gives you an idea of how harsh and insurmountable the wilderness of Papua can be. The group of Japanese soldiers Samuel encountered, of which only one (Iwataro Hayashi) was still alive at the time, was a small portion of these unfortunate men.

Why did Samuel give Lamotelokhai clay to the dying Japanese soldier? Samuel had been deeply troubled by the terrible massacre of Penapul's tribe. He felt responsible for it. In a way, perhaps he *was* responsible, although he did not intend for it to happen. Since being captured by Sinanie's tribe, Samual had struggled to understand the importance of the human characteristic of compassion. In fact, he was beginning to wonder of his sophisticated London society had less compassion than the tribe in which he found himself a captive. Samuel had decided that it was his responsibility to become more compassionate. In 1944, when he came upon the almost-dead soldier (Iwataro Hayashi), he felt a need to show compassion, so he treated the man with the clay of the Lamotelokhai.

Does that mean Iwataro Hayashi survived and became immortal? Maybe. We don't really know. Iwataro does not appear later on in the **Diffusion** series. I have often toyed with the idea of writing a story of what happened to Iwataro Hayashi after his encounter with Samuel.

What did Samuel mean when he said, "We must all become improved?" Samuel believed the world was not ready for the Lamotelokhai. He had decided that compassion was the last— perhaps unobtainable—goal to be achieved by any advanced civilization. Without a broad, general sense of compassion that is ubiquitous throughout humanity, the Lamotelokhai will inevitably be used inappropriately, perhaps even resulting in the demise of all civilization.

Do you really believe taking the Lamotelokhai out of the wilderness and making it available to the world would result in disaster? Personally, I do believe this is likely. Why? Because compassion is not found in abundance in the heart of every human being. It is abundant in many people, but obviously not in everyone. Actually, I am an optimist at heart. I believe things will get better, and people will become kinder to each other. But at this point in time, we may not be ready for the

Lamotelokhai. If you want a startling image of what might happen, be sure to read **Profusion** (after you have read **Diffusion** and **Infusion**, of course).

What is the significance of the title **Savage**? This title refers to the intellectual dilemma faced by Samuel. The more he learned about Sinanie's tribe, and the more he contemplated the nature of the supposedly civilized society from which he had come, the more he began to wonder who was the Savage. After all, regarding the massacre of Penapul's tribe, Samuel later realized that he may have been able to save many of those men, but he had chosen not to act. Who is more savage? Is it the relatively uncivilized indigenous people he once looked down upon, or is it Samuel himself?

I'll close with a few more important things.

First, I must say that I have the deepest respect for the unique cultures of the Papuan peoples. Obviously I have taken liberties in developing the characteristics of Sinanie's tribe, but I intended no disrespect by doing so. I have also taken some liberties in developing Penapul's tribe, although nearly all of their characteristics are based upon actual Papuan cultures, as described by Alfred Russell Wallace in his amazing account of his work in that part of the world from 1854 to 1862, titled *The Malay Archipelago* (first published in 1869), and as described by other authors listed below.

I must also remind you that the character Samuel Inwood was a product of his time. His notions and ideals are based on an accumulation of research and reading the texts of such men as

Alfred Wallace. It is not my intention to insult the more modern sensibilities of readers. Instead, I wish to accurately depict a man of Samuel's time and station in life, and his gradual realization of a broader way of looking at humanity.

I adapted the language of Sinanie's tribe from the amazing work of Gerrit J. van Enk and Lourens de Vries in their studies of the language and culture of the Korowai, a Papuan community of treehouse dwellers of southern Irian Jaya (now called Papua). Astoundingly, the Korowai had never come into contact with outsiders until the early 1980s.

I was thrilled to find two books that helped me immensely with phrases and slang used in the mid 1800s. Both of these are delightful reference books, and I highly recommend them. The first is *Passing English of the Victorian Era: a Dictionary of Heterodox English, Slang and Phrase* (by James Redding Ware, first published in 1909). The second is *The Routledge Dictionary of Historical Slang* (by Eric Partridge, published in 1973).

I am thankful for the hard work of those who have painstakingly researched the cultures, wildlife, and ecosystems of Papua. The following are recommended books (and one video).

Flannery, Tim. *Mammals of New Guinea*. Chatswood, New South Wales: Reed Books Australia, 1995. Print.

Flannery, Tim. *Throwim Way Leg: Tree Kangaroos, Possums, and Penis Gourds – On the Track of Unknown Mammals in*

Wildest New Guinea. New York: Atlantic Monthly Press, 1998. Print.

Marriott, Edward. *The Lost Tribe – A Harrowing Passage into New Guinea's Heart of Darkness.* New York: Henry Holt and Company, 1996. Print.

Merrifield, William, Gregerson, Marilyn, and Ajamiseba, Daniel, Ed. *Gods, Heroes, Kinsmen: Ethnographic Studies from Irian Jaya, Indonesia.* Jayapura, Irian Jaya: Cenderawasih University, 1983. Print.

Muller, Kal. *New Guinea: Journey Into the Stone Age.* Lincolnwood, Illinois: Passport Books, 1997. Print.

Souter, Gavin. *New Guinea: The Last Unknown.* New York: Taplinger Publishing, 1966. Print.

Van Enk, Gerrit J. and de Vries, Lourens. *The Korowai of Irian Jaya – Their Language in its Cultural Context.* New York: Oxford University Press, 1997. Print.

Wallace, Alfred Russell. *The Malay Archipelago.* 1869. Print or ebook.
This astounding work, which is in two volumes, is now in the public domain and can be found in a variety of print and ebook formats. If you are at all interested in the exploration of this part of the world, I highly recommend reading Wallace's work.

Sky Above Mud Below. Dir. and Perf. Pierre-Dominique Gaisseau (organizer and leader) and Gerard Delloye (assistant leader). Lorimar Home Video, 1962. VHS.

This is an amazing video filmed as it happened in 1959, when a group of explorers set out on a seven-month attempt to cross the jungles of Papua (then called Dutch New Guinea). Winner of the 1961 Academy Award for Best Documentary Feature.

ACKNOWLEDGMENTS

I am not capable of creating a book such as this on my own. I have the following people, among others, to thank for their assistance.

When it comes to editing, my son Micheal Smith is extremely talented, and his tireless and meticulous suggestions are invaluable. If you find a sentence or detail in the book that doesn't seem right, it is likely because I failed to implement one of his suggestions.

My wife, Trish, is always the first to read my work, and therefore she has the burden of seeing my stories in their roughest form. Thankfully, she does not hesitate to point out where things are a mess. Her suggestions are what get the editing process started. She also helps with various promotional efforts. And finally, she not only tolerates my obsession with writing, she actually encourages it.

Monique Agueros, a colleague of mine for many years, also provided helpful editing suggestions.

I am thankful to all the independent freelance designers

out there who provide quality work for independent authors such as myself. The mostly hand-drawn map of New Guinea at the beginning of the book was created by Sabrina Genarri (via fiverr.com). The awesome cover design was created by J. Caleb Clark (www.jcalebdesign.com).

ABOUT THE AUTHOR

Stan Smith has lived most of his life in the Midwest United States and currently resides with his wife Trish in a home nestled within an Ozark forest near Warsaw, Missouri. He writes adventure novels and short stories that have a generous sprinkling of science fiction. His novels and stories are about regular people who find themselves caught up in highly unusual situations. They are designed to stimulate your sense of wonder, get your heart pounding, and keep you reading late into the night, with minimal risk of exposure to spelling and punctuation errors. His books are for anyone who loves adventure, discovery, and mind-bending surprises.

Stan's Author Website
http://www.stancsmith.com

Feel free to email Stan at: stan@stancsmith.com
He loves hearing from readers and will answer every email.

ALSO BY STAN C. SMITH

The DIFFUSION series

Diffusion

Infusion

Profusion

Savage

Blue Arrow

Diffusion Box Set

The BRIDGERS series

Bridgers 1: The Lure of Infinity

Bridgers 2: The Cost of Survival

Bridgers 3: The Voice of Reason

Bridgers 4: The Mind of Many

Bridgers 5: The Trial of Extinction

Bridgers 6: The Bond of Absolution

INFINITY: A Bridger's Origin

Bridgers 1-3 Box Set

Bridgers 4-6 Box Set

The ACROSS HORIZONS series

1: Obsolete Theorem

2. Foregone Conflict

3. Hostile Emergence

Stand-alone Stories

Parthenium's Year